Norah paused to st[...] ver frame on a cry[...] It was an eight-by-ten glossy of a young woman in evening dress. Her face was a perfect oval, her brow high and clear, her eyes large and luminous, her dark hair coiled around her head. The gown was heavy satin, its bodice encrusted with glittering stones and pearls. She held herself like a princess.

Stepping over the threshold, Norah entered an oasis of summer in the midst of the snow. The pool was of Olympian proportions, its blue waters sparkling in the sun that flooded through the transparent dome. Trees, shrubs and flowers in redwood tubs turned it into a bower. Wrought-iron furniture with bright cushions invited lounging.

And at the center of it all, floating lazily in the scintillating water, dark hair spread around her head—was the victim. Facedown . . .

A
GOOD NIGHT
TO
KILL

Lillian O'Donnell

FAWCETT CREST • NEW YORK

A Fawcett Crest Book
Published by Ballantine Books
Copyright © 1989 by Lillian O'Donnell

Library of Congress Catalog Card Number: 88-11552

ISBN 0-449-21706-X

This edition published by arrangement with G.P. Putnam's
Sons, a division of the Putnam Berkley Group, Inc.

Manufactured in the United States of America

First Ballantine Books Edition: January 1990

He looked for justice, but behold bloodshed;
for righteousness, but behold, a cry!

ISAIAH 5:7

CHAPTER ONE

The snow started just after four in the afternoon. At first a few scattered flakes wafted gently down, melting as soon as they struck the pavement. By five, it had thickened and a light mantle covered the fields and paths of Central Park; the streets outside, though wet, were still bare.

In her basement bookshop on Seventieth off Columbus, Stefanie Altman packed mail orders and listened to the weather reports over the radio. The prediction was for accumulations of twelve to eighteen inches in the northern suburbs and as much as eight to ten in the city. The wind was expected to reach blizzard velocity. Offices were closing early and everyone was urged to get home as soon as possible. And stay there. Watching the people scurry past the shop, Stefanie Altman decided to heed the advice.

She was twenty-three, a plain, shy girl, only child of a dentist in Manchester, Vermont. Her brown hair was silky but hung straight and limp, hiding most of her narrow face so that she seemed to be peering out from behind a curtain. Her hazel eyes were large; magnified by thick lenses, they dominated her face. She wore the long, loose garments she thought were still in fashion and they made her look more vague and unfocused than she actually was.

For Stefanie Altman had changed since fleeing her hometown. In Manchester she'd never had a boyfriend, not even anybody to take her to her own high school prom. Marriage and a family seemed out of her reach. No disgrace in our present time, if one had a talent or skill to compensate. Stefanie did not. She couldn't bear to stay and be pitied or patronized. In a big city, in New York, she would be anonymous. She got a job in a big company whose name and product were household words, and discovered that a big company is very much like a small town. Everybody knows everybody else and the same standards apply; the same gossip circulates; the same judgments are passed. Though she changed jobs three times, Stefanie Altman found herself always a misfit. It was as she was scanning the employment pages of the *Times* for yet another situation that her eye caught the Business Opportunities section. There were all kinds of businesses for sale. She looked over the offerings casually—skipped the franchises, passed over the mail-order "opportunities." A humble, three-line ad jumped out at her: *Neighborhood bookstore.*

She'd always been an avid reader. As she was an introverted only child, books had been companionship and stimulus for her imagination. They provided color and excitement in her life. She noted the store was located only six blocks from where she lived. No more subways and buses, she thought, her heart pounding. She had a small inheritance from her parents, which she hadn't touched so far. She had talked herself into buying the place before she even saw it.

Two steps down from the street, its door set in a brick-faced arch and flanked by a pair of evergreens in tubs, the store was everything she'd known it would be. A brass bell over the door tinkled as she opened it and brought goose bumps of pleasure. Inside, it was snug—three narrow rooms opening one into the next under a low ceiling— warmed with solid built-in oaken bookcases and gloriously cluttered with books, to read, to sell, to gloat over.

She barely glanced at the accounts. Oh, she was aware the store was losing money, but it didn't matter. The couple running it were old, she reasoned; they weren't putting in the effort. She was young, willing to work; she would make a success of it. She started by running a lending library for those who couldn't afford to buy and by giving discounts wherever possible to those who could. She encouraged browsing. She was ready to discuss books, to help make a selection. She adjusted her store hours to the needs of her customers, which meant opening around noon and not closing till at least 10:00 P.M. She kept a large coffee urn going. The store became a neighborhood meeting place. But nobody would drop by tonight, Stefanie Altman thought as she looked out at the thickening snow.

She put on a long, down-filled coat, boots, a knitted wool cap and matching scarf. Keys in hand, she hesitated over the cash box. After four break-ins, she made it a habit never to leave money overnight, but today she'd made only one sale and the night depository was two blocks out of her way. Let it go; the few dollars would serve to make change tomorrow, she decided, and put the box back in the drawer. The gun, however, she took out and placed in the deep right-hand pocket of the storm coat where she could feel its reassuring bulk against her thigh.

The doorbell rang.

She looked up and, through the falling curtain of white, made out a familiar face. Smiling with pleasure she buzzed in Timothy Kampel.

"I was just closing."

"I figured you would be, so I came by to invite you to the opera."

Tim Kampel was typical of her customers: young, ambitious, eager to stretch his mind. Days he worked as a teller at the neighborhood branch of Citibank, and he moonlighted as a waiter at the Grand Tier Restaurant of the Metropolitan Opera House. "I figure the house will be half empty on a night like this. It'll be no trouble getting you in. After, we can have a snack somewhere." He was twenty-six, short, bandy-legged. He had frizzy dark hair and an incongruous handlebar mustache. He talked loudly and dressed garishly because underneath he was as shy as Stefanie.

"It's *Don Giovanni,*" he informed her, Mozart being the ultimate inducement as far as he was concerned. "What do you say, Stefie?"

Lately, he'd taken to coming over after he was through at the restaurant and waiting till she closed and then walking her home. Sometimes, they stopped for a bite, but they'd never had a formal date. She'd been expecting him to get up the nerve, but now that he had, Stefanie felt oddly reluctant.

"It's such a bad night."

"That's the point. It would be standing room only otherwise."

"Of course. And I'd love to go, Tim, but I honestly don't feel up to it. I'm still kind of shook from the last . . . incident. You know?" She realized that it was true; she was still very nervous. "Another time? Will you ask me another time?"

"If you want," he said glumly.

"I do. Oh, I do."

"Well then, sure, you bet. Okay." He grinned. "I'll walk you home."

"If it won't make you late for work."

"I've got an excuse." He nodded toward the snow outside and winked.

With Tim beside her while she locked up, there was no need for Stefanie Altman to cast surreptitious looks over her shoulder to make sure nobody was loitering. Also, she wasn't carrying any cash. So for now, the constant anxiety eased as she took his arm and they set out together.

Conditioned by the dire tone of the forecaster, Stefie was surprised that it was actually pleasant outside. True, the snow had intensified, but the wind was calm, for now at least. There were few people on the street, these quite evidently getting home as fast as they could. Only the occasional car clanked and wheezed laboriously by. The loneliness and unaccustomed quiet was also reassuring. At the corner of Columbus, Stefie stopped. "You go on to your job, Tim. I'll be okay."

"Are you sure?"

"I am. Just don't wait for another storm before asking me out again. All right?"

Timothy Kampel looked hard at her, then he swooped. She thought he was going to kiss her; instead he grabbed her hand and pumped it. "All right. Well, all right. Thank you." He turned and darted across the street. From there he waved once more and disappeared into the white mists.

She was alone.

One block over, Central Park West was composed of an unbroken row of massive apartment buildings, some fine examples of Art Deco and Neo-Gothic, but most undistinguished except for size. The side streets, however, were made up of small residences usually not more than five stories high, an architectural hodgepodge. There were columned entrances, elaborate pediments, grinning gargoyles, fretted ironwork. In the rapidly failing twilight and mantled in white, it all looked like a turn-of-the-century village.

The snow had begun to stick and formed a carpet that muffled steps, so Stefanie sensed the presence behind her rather than heard it. When she looked around all she could make out was an indistinct figure—thick torso and pipe-stem legs, like one of those Don Quixote sculptures you could buy for five dollars or five thousand. The wind was gusting again and the flurries seemed to swirl around the man so that at moments he was clearly there and at others gone. Just somebody like herself trying to get home, Stefanie thought, and walked faster.

She turned her corner and was a quarter of the way up the block before looking to see if he was still behind her. But now instead of one there were two. And as she looked, a third figure materialized. She had no idea from where, only that there were three. She shivered, but it had nothing to do with her leaking boots. She began to run.

"Hey, Miss! Lady? Wait a second," one of them, the tallest, the one she'd seen first, called. "Wait up, will you?"

She pretended she didn't hear and kept on going.

"Can you tell me the way to the nearest subway?" he shouted.

Reaching the foot of the stairs of her brownstone, she stopped. Hesitated. Caught her breath. "I'm sorry, I don't know." She threw it over her shoulder and started up.

"What? What did you say?"

"I said I don't know. I'm sorry."

By now Stefanie had reached the landing and was at her own front door. The three men stood at the bottom of the stairs.

"I asked you a civil question," the tall one persisted. "You could give a civil answer."

"I told you I don't know. I'm sorry."

"You could at least look at me when you talk to me."

She had her house keys in her hand but she was shaking so hard she dropped them in the snow.

Instantly, or so it seemed, with his long legs taking the steps two at a time, he was up there with her, had found the keys and picked them up. "So maybe you could lend us cab fare? We're lost. We don't know the way home. Ten dollars should do it. What do you say, guys? Ten bucks okay?"

He was wearing a ski mask. It was red wool and covered his entire face with a slot for the eyes only. She looked into those light blue eyes and as she did she heard the others laugh. The laughter was the most frightening of all that had happened so far. She forced herself to look away from the man who confronted her to search the street. There was nobody out. Nothing moved. People were at home. They sat snug behind lighted windows. If she screamed would anybody behind those closed windows and doors even hear her?

"I'm sorry, I don't have ten dollars."

"Come on, lady, ten bucks. For your key."

"I haven't got ten dollars. I told you. Go away. Leave me alone. I haven't got it."

"Let's not make a big deal out of this, lady. You give

us whatever you've got—watch, jewelry, a pretty ring . . . don't make us take it from you."

"Go away." Stefanie took a step back and felt the weight of the gun in her pocket.

The man in the mask took a step forward. She reached inside.

A shot rang out.

His knees buckled. Another shot. He sank to the ground in front of her.

For uncounted seconds Stefanie Altman was aware only of the figure huddled at her feet. Then, as she watched in horror, he rolled over slowly on his side and down one step, then over and down another, gathering momentum till he tumbled all the way down the entire flight to the pavement. There he lay still.

Another pause. One of the two at the bottom of the stairs, a squat man in a duffel coat with a wool cap pulled low, shuffled over to the still form. He sighed heavily. "You better call an ambulance."

Dazed, Stefanie Altman looked at the gun in her hand.

"You shot him!" the other, younger and wearing a ski mask, shouted. "You shot him." His voice rose stridently. "You didn't have to do that." His eyes glistened with hatred. "Bitch. Bitch! You'll be sorry," he cried out.

"Go away," Stefanie moaned. "Go away." Tears ran down her cheeks as she raised the gun again.

The two men ran.

She fired wildly, again and again, till they both disappeared down the street. The shots echoed and reechoed.

Silence returned slowly. The lights in the buildings glowed steadily. No shades were raised, no curtain parted. The man down on the sidewalk didn't move. After a while, when she thought her legs would support her, Stefanie Altman, leaning heavily on the rail, walked down to him. She crossed the sidewalk warily. He didn't move. She knelt in the snow beside him, and those blue eyes now stared at her through the slit in the mask with a terrible sightless gaze. Nevertheless, she had to check the carotid artery as she had been taught in CPR class. To do that, she would have to take the mask off him. She put the gun back in her pocket, and with one hand on the crown of his head and the other gripping the neck band, she part pulled and part rolled the mask off. At the final yank, his head rolled to one side as though he were turning away from her. But she had seen enough.

"Oh, God! My God, what have I done?"

CHAPTER
TWO

As the snow intensified, the city wound down. Trains and buses crawled. Private cars stalled and were abandoned to be buried in drifts. Commuters were stranded. In another hour it would be impossible to move except underground. It was a good night to sit home by the hearth, or its modern equivalent—the TV set, Simon Wyler thought, looking idly out the window of the squad room at the Eighty-second Street station house. He anticipated a quiet shift; muggers and likely victims, pushers and anxious buyers would have the sense to stay inside.

Of the detectives who had gone out since the snow started only a handful had made it back and they didn't expect to be going out again. Paperwork and odd jobs were being cleaned up. The atmosphere was relaxed. When the phone rang on his desk, Simon Wyler assumed it was Lola, his current girlfriend.

Detective First Grade Simon Wyler was twenty-nine. He had eight years on the force, four of them as a detective and the last two in his present rank as a member of Homicide, Fourth Division. He was six foot two, slim, jaunty. His face was narrow, nose aquiline, gray eyes set slightly too close together. It gave him an inquisitive look—not a bad thing in his line of work. His dark hair was wavy and swept back from a perfect widow's peak, the length reaching to the top of his shirt collar. He was known as a stylish dresser, his current taste being for long, narrow topcoats and wide-brimmed "Indiana Jones" fedoras— pale cream in summer, soft Alpine green in winter. He looked more like one of the new breed of MBAs that were invading Wall Street than a police detective. Though he'd had a couple of live-in "relationships," Simon Wyler had never been married. However, he was seriously contemplating legitimizing his current affair. His eyes were alight as he picked up the phone.

But it wasn't Lola. Homicide, apparently, had not been put on hold by the weather, Wyler thought as he jotted down the details relayed by Communications. According to the report of the Radio Motor Patrol (RMP) officer at the scene, it was open and shut and the "perp" was actually in custody. Nevertheless, when Wyler hung up he took time to consider. Under the dashing exterior, Simon Wyler was a thorough, patient investigator. Ordinarily, the case in hand was not one he would refer to the "Lieut," not at this stage, but in the context of today's blurred line between criminal and victim . . . Simon Wyler left his desk and made his way to the squad commander's office. He knocked.

"Come."

Lieutenant Mulcahaney was going through the current batch of DD5s, Detective Detailed Reports. In a year and a half as head of Homicide, Fourth Division, Norah Mulcahaney had reached professional and personal maturity. Physically, she was at her peak. Her clear white skin showed only traces of lines at the eyes and mouth. Her dark hair was lustrous and abundant; her deep blue eyes bright and searching. From an overweight, shy girl she had developed into a slim and handsome woman. She carried herself with the assurance of her rank. True, there were light shadows under her eyes and a frown was etched between her thick eyebrows, perhaps to compensate for the set of her square, prominent jaw—a bellwether of her mood—which had taken on a less stubborn, less aggressive thrust.

Norah took off the glasses she now needed for reading and brushed back a strand of hair that had escaped from the green silk scarf with which she'd tied it back. She was tired, but only from an accumulation of work, nothing out of the ordinary. She was looking forward to a quiet family dinner at her sister-in-law Lena's place in Brooklyn. After that, she had two days off in the rotation. She needed them.

She looked up. "What've you got?"

"Homicide on Seventy-sixth," Wyler told her. "Started as a mugging and ended with the victim killing her assailant."

The frown deepened instantly. Norah stifled a sigh. There were too many of these occurrences lately, too many instances in which the roles reversed and victim and assailant changed places. Each case had to be handled with care, rights carefully observed, or the police officer and the department could be caught in a crossfire.

She put away the file she'd been working on and got up, looking out the window as she opened her locker. "It's coming down hard."

"Maybe we should leave the cars and go by subway?" Wyler suggested.

They decided to walk.

Coming out into a world of white and cold, Norah Mulcahaney felt an instant exhilaration. Snow came infrequently to the city and the occasions on which it came in significant amounts were memorable. As she and Simon Wyler bent their heads into the wind, which by now was gusting and brought tears to their eyes, there was no possibility for conversation, so she could indulge her memories—

Norah was thirteen; her mother had been dead only four months and she was keeping house for her father and two older brothers, Patrick Junior and Edward. After a storm much like this, Patrick Senior had caught his only daughter looking wistfully out the window. In that moment he realized the heavy burden he had allowed her to take on. He ordered all chores set aside. He got her and the boys bundled up and took them sleigh riding in Central Park. Norah never forgot the magic of that day—the frozen lake, the white, crystalline tracery of trees against a brilliant sky, the laughter of the other children on the big hill on Seventy-second Street. It was the first time since her mother's death the family had joined in anything other than weeping.

The second recollection was of a trip she and Joe took to the Laurentian Mountains in Canada. Norah was no athlete, in fact she took no physical exercise at all until she was forced to do so as part of her training at the police academy. But skiing came instinctively. She felt the rhythm of the turns, rose up and shifted down, adjusted to the terrain, glowed with the sense of the efficiency of her own body. That trip, those times on the mountain were among the happiest of their marriage. Looking back, she realized the six years she and Joe Capretto, Captain Joseph Antony Capretto of the NYPD, were together were few in proportion to the rest of her life, yet the influence of the marriage kept growing. Joe was gone, brutally killed in the line of duty, but his memory didn't fade. Norah's strength, determination, dedication were her own, but Joe had taught her to keep things in perspective. He had seen to it that she leavened work with other interests. Joe had taught her to laugh.

She still missed him. Oh, God! she missed him. But the cruel pain had abated. At first, her instinct had been to run away—from everything: the home they'd shared, even the Job. She took a leave of absence and found a house in the Amish country, but she carried the past with her. She tried the reverse and immersed herself in her work. No good either. Loneliness was an opponent. She fought it. She almost fell in love. Almost. In the end, Norah was the one who walked away; she was the one not willing to make the commitment. And after the breakup with Gary Reissig, she was more alone than ever.

Then Norah met a young policewoman, a rookie, Audrey Jordan. Officer Jordan reminded Norah very much of herself when she first joined the force. She invited Audrey to move in with her. Because of her responsibilities at home, Norah Mulcahaney had never had a close girlfriend. She'd never giggled in corners with another girl, done homework with her, exchanged confidences, talked about boys. Unfortunately, Audrey, as the child of itinerant actors always on the move, hadn't either. Neither one knew how to help the other to a true friendship.

They might have reached it through shared interest in the work, but it soon became apparent that Audrey wasn't meant to be a cop. Norah tried to help, tried to push Audrey in the path she had followed, but Audrey was not her clone. She wanted to find her own way and when she did, she discovered it didn't involve police work. So Audrey Jordan resigned. The last Norah had heard she was out on the Coast with her parents and had a small part in a daytime soap.

Once again Norah was alone. Finally she stopped fighting the solitude and settled for a truce. She accepted there would be empty hours and, like most single working women in the city, learned to fill them—with theaters, movies, hobbies, casual friends. She adjusted. She achieved a balance. And she was happy. Not in the way she had been with Joe. That could not be again, but she stopped trying to duplicate him.

The familiar wail of the siren broke into her reverie and the EMS van skidding around the corner brought her back to the present.

The scene might differ, Norah thought, but the basic components didn't change. About a quarter of the way up the block, yellow plastic rope had already been strung to mark the crime area. Norah and Wyler approached the uniform on guard.

"What've you got, George?"

"Hi, Lieutenant," George Franciscus greeted Norah.

He was a big, overweight man, five years on the force and a plodder. It was not likely he would ever rise in rank, but he performed carefully and honestly within his abilities. Franciscus now produced a much-worn notebook and thumbed to the latest entry.

"Ms. Stefanie Altman, residing right here"—he indicated the brownstone directly behind them—"was coming home from work when she realized she was being followed. She walked as fast as she could, but the man caught up with her. He accosted her and asked for money. She told him she didn't have any. He insisted. She was so frightened she dropped her keys in the snow. He got them and refused to return them unless she gave him ten dollars. She thought he was going to assault her so she pulled her gun."

"Hold it, George. Did you read her her rights?" Norah asked.

"You bet, Lieutenant. The minute she mentioned pulling the gun."

"Good. Go on."

"She fired and he went down. She had no idea she'd killed him, she said. She never meant to do anything but scare him off." The cop paused, squinted at his own scrawl, and tilted the notebook toward the streetlight for a better look. "Oh, yeah, she doesn't have a license to carry."

Norah exchanged a quick glance with Wyler. "I assume you took possession of the piece?"

"Yes, ma'am. I turned it over to Forensics." He closed his book, indicating that on the next point he didn't need refreshing. "She only mentioned one shot, but the clip was empty."

"Make?"

"A .32 Beretta automatic."

"And who called in the complaint? Ms. Altman?"

"No, a neighbor." Franciscus needed his book again. "Clarence Hurt. Resides in the same building as the perpetrator."

Norah winced. "You mean Ms. Altman."

Franciscus flushed. "Sorry, Lieutenant."

"How about the man she shot?" Norah asked, not willing to put a label on either one yet. "What've you got on him?"

"Driver's license in the name of Frank Beech, Staten Island. No credit cards. He did have a social security ID."

Norah looked over to the knot of men surrounding the body of Frank Beech. "Where's Ms. Altman?"

"I sent her and Hurt inside. The two of them were standing out here waiting when we arrived. I thought, what with the weather and all, it would be okay. My partner, Sid Weeks, is with them, though I suppose if they wanted to cook up anything they had plenty of time to do it before we got here."

Norah looked hard at him. "You have a reason to suspect they might have?"

"Just following procedure, Lieutenant."

"Okay, thanks, George."

With Wyler still at her side, Norah approached the medical examiner, who was still conducting the preliminary examination. "I'm Lieutenant Mulcahaney and this is Detective Wyler, Fourth Homicide, Dr. Jasper." Though they hadn't met yet, she knew who he was. "What can you tell us?"

Dominick Jasper was in his late thirties and already balding. He was of medium height and weight, with a round, mild face to which a wispy beard added little distinction. He was bareheaded. His London Fog raincoat and shell rubbers were totally inadequate to the conditions. She wondered what he'd been doing when he got the call.

Jasper got up and shook hands cordially. "We have here a male Caucasian, twenty-five to twenty-eight years of age. Shot twice—once through the front of the left shoulder and once through the heart. That was instantly fatal."

He was pleasant and direct and not trying to impress with technicalese, Norah thought. She liked that. It suggested he was confident but not a showoff. Then she considered the information. Two shots. "How come he's lying facedown?" she asked.

Jasper shrugged. "The impact of the first shot caused him to turn away instinctively."

"That would be the shot in the shoulder, since the one through the heart was instantly fatal?"

"Yes. All right."

"But if he was already turning, wouldn't the second shot have hit him in the side or even the back?"

"Assuming the shots were fired in rapid succession, and I think that's a fair assumption, the body reaction—actually, the reflex—that jerked him around and made him fall forward came not between the shots but after."

"I see. Mind if we take a look, Dr. Jasper?"

"Please." Jasper stepped to one side.

The first thing Norah noticed as she knelt beside the fallen man was that the blanket of snow that had been disturbed by the RMP team and now the assistant medical examiner was rapidly forming again. Nevertheless, the exit wound in his back was readily apparent. She could see no similar wound in the region of his left shoulder.

"Okay to turn him over?"

"The photographers are through, so it's your pleasure, Lieutenant." Jasper stamped his feet.

Freezing, Norah thought, and anxious to get somewhere warm. Too bad; she wasn't going to be rushed. With Wyler's help, she turned Beech over, faceup. Jasper had put him in his mid to late twenties. Norah thought he might have been a bit younger. His skin was coarse, and, even allowing for the pallor of death, suggested that he spent little time outdoors. His hair was dark and straight and he wore a dark, thin mustache. Below it, in contrast, his lips were thick, sensual. In fact, he wasn't bad-looking, Norah thought. He might even have been handsome. He was wearing jeans, poor quality, and the down jacket was cheap. It was soaked more by the slush in which he'd been lying than blood.

"Would the cold affect the rate of bleeding?" Norah asked Jasper.

"After death? Somewhat."

He was becoming more cautious in his answers, Norah

thought. She noted the red wool ski mask lying beside the body. "How about that? Who took it off him?"

"Officer Franciscus stated the mask was off and lying beside the body when he and his partner arrived," Jasper replied.

Carefully, Norah and Wyler eased Beech back to the original position. On her feet again, Norah took a slow look around. The snow in the immediate vicinity had been trampled, undoubtedly by the police. It could hardly have been avoided. The snow on the steps, on the stoop, and in front of the brownstone entrance indicated there had been activity there too. Whether or not that was attributable to the police, the continuing fall had just about wiped out any story the tracks might have told.

"Can you estimate the distance from which the shots were fired?" Norah asked Jasper.

"Not until I get a good look at the entry wounds."

"How about the time of death?"

"In this weather?" he demanded. "I can't even guess. Not yet. You have the woman who did it in custody."

Norah ignored that. "I assume the snow under him melted because of body heat. It hasn't frozen again yet," she pointed out.

"Calculations based on body temperature are approximate at best, as you surely know."

Norah nodded. "So that's it?"

"I don't know what else you can expect at this time, Lieutenant."

"Dr. Jasper, I was only asking."

"All right. When we get him on the table we'll pay special attention to the possibility of powder burns. But if your people could locate the bullet that passed through him, we could figure the trajectory and that would be a better way to establish the distance."

So the ball was back in her court, Norah thought. "We'll give it a try, Dr. Jasper. Count on it."

He pressed his lips into a tight line. "Lieutenant, it's an open-and-shut case, for God's sake. What's your problem?"

"My problem is that you've accounted for two shots, but the gun has an eight-round capability. Its clip was empty."

Certainly it was possible that the gun wasn't fully loaded, Norah knew that; still the likelihood was that it had had more than two rounds in it. Somebody must have heard the shots, she thought. The neighbor who had called in the complaint, at least. Somebody else might even have looked out. People were watching now, Norah thought. She could sense it. A canvass of the neighbors should be undertaken immediately while events were still fresh in the memory, before the pervasive fear of "getting involved" hardened into stubborn resistance, or before memory was distorted and became self-serving. She had to get a team over here right away.

Mentally sorting through those available, Norah chose three new men, Neel, Ochs, and Tedesco, and sent Wyler to call the squad for them. Danny Neel came from three generations of cops; he was also a college graduate. Julius Ochs was studying law in his spare time. Nicolo Tedesco was the father of four and while he lacked the formal education of the others, he had a natural shrewdness. In addition, each one had a skill that couldn't be learned—each one knew how to handle people.

Norah waited for Wyler to return before entering the brownstone. Together they went to Stefanie Altman's apartment. Wyler had caught the squeal; he was carrying the case; Norah intended to defer to him in the interrogation.

The first thing Wyler did was to have Officer Weeks escort Clarence Hurt, the neighbor who had been sitting with Stefanie Altman, to his own apartment. "We'll look in on you shortly," he said. Then he turned his full attention to the girl.

She was sitting at the end of the sofa, drawn, bedraggled. The coat she'd been wearing was tossed on a chair and dark patches of melted snow still showed. The wool cap on top of it was also damp.

"Is there anything I can get you, Ms. Altman? Coffee? A glass of water?"

"No, thank you."

"You do understand, Ms. Altman, that you are not required by law to answer any questions at this time?"

She nodded, but her large myopic eyes were fixed on Norah. "You're a policewoman? A lieutenant?"

"Yes, I am."

She said no more but went on staring at Norah.

"Officer Franciscus did read you your rights?" Wyler pressed.

"Yes, yes!" she finally stopped looking at Norah and glared at him. "Why are you making such a big thing out of it? I don't understand why I have to have my rights read to me. I didn't do anything wrong. I'm not the criminal. He is." She caught herself. "He was. He was the criminal. He followed me. He threatened me. He and his buddies. All the way up from Columbus Avenue." Her face was flushed. She reverted to Norah.

"He wanted money. I didn't have any. Then he wanted my watch and jewelry. What was I supposed to do?" Her appeal was now open and direct.

Norah hesitated. Mugging victims were routinely advised not to resist, to hand over money and valuables—and save their lives. Maybe it was cynical, but it was also realistic, though now was hardly the time to point that out. "Did he threaten you with bodily harm?" she asked gently.

"He said: 'Don't make me take them away from you.' "

"And you understood that to mean he intended to use force?"

"Of course. What else? What would you think if three men surrounded you and demanded money?"

"Three?" Wyler decided it was time to pick up on the numbers. "In your statement to Officer Franciscus you mention only one."

"Oh? Is that right? I don't remember. Anyway, there were three. I swear." Her color deepened to an unhealthy scarlet.

A look from Norah warned Wyler to let it go for now. "Okay, Ms. Altman, why don't you just tell us about it in your own words?"

Stefanie Altman swallowed. Her color subsided. "I have a bookstore on Seventieth near Columbus. I closed early tonight because of the storm. I guess it was a little after five. A friend walked me part of the way home. On Columbus we parted. After maybe a couple of blocks, I got the feeling I was being followed. I looked back and saw a man. I looked back a couple of times but he seemed to be keeping his distance. I told myself he was just heading for home like I was. I told myself I was getting paranoid because of everything that's happened to me lately."

She paused, but Wyler didn't prompt. He'd worked with the lieut long enough to know she wanted a witness to have as much rein as possible.

"I tried to ignore him," Stefanie Altman went on, the words coming more easily. "But every time I looked back there he was. When I got to my corner, suddenly there were two other men with him. I don't know where they came from; visibility was awful—just suddenly they were there with him. I was really scared. I tried to run, but it was very slippery. I managed to get to my house and up the stairs to the front door. I was so nervous, I dropped my keys. He, the first one, was right behind me and picked them up. He wouldn't give them to me. He wanted me to buy them back. His buddies thought it was a great joke. They laughed." She stopped expectantly.

And now, clearly, she did need prompting. "Did the first man, the one who made the demands, did he laugh too?" Wyler asked.

"You think because they were laughing there was no need to be afraid? Believe me, there was. Look, this isn't the first time I've been threatened. Four times in the last three months my store has been broken into. Twice, I was still there and I was held at gunpoint. The police aren't helping me. Nobody's helping me. I understand you're spread thin, Lieutenant. I understand you can't post a guard in every store and every building, but I couldn't even get a permit to carry a gun. The reason I was turned down was *insufficient need*. Just what *is* sufficient need, Lieutenant?"

Norah had no answer for her.

"What was I supposed to do? What? You tell me, Detective Wyler. You tell me, Lieutenant."

She had done the only thing she could and gone out and got herself a weapon illegally. Their silence acknowledged it.

"I'm sorry I killed him. I'm honestly and deeply sorry. I never meant to. I swear to you, I swear to God, I never meant to kill him."

She had reached the limit of her endurance and for a fleeting moment it seemed that she had lost control. Then she called on the remnants of her strength and will.

"I would never have taken the gun out of my pocket if he hadn't pulled the knife first."

"Knife, Ms. Altman?" Wyler asked. "You didn't mention he had a knife."

"Didn't I? Everything happened so fast. I'm sorry."

"Where did he have the knife?"

"You mean where did he get it from? I don't know. I didn't notice. From his sleeve maybe. I'm not sure. All I know is he was holding it and pointing the blade at me."

Again Wyler had to prompt. "And then?"

The girl shook her head in bewilderment. "I don't know; he was down in the snow at my feet. Then, after a couple of seconds, he rolled over down the stairs to the sidewalk. I don't remember firing, but I suppose I did. I had the gun in my hand."

"You shot him twice," Wyler told her.

"I don't remember."

"Did you carry a full clip?" Wyler asked.

She sighed. "No. I was advised it wasn't necessary. It was half full."

"It's empty now, so you must have fired four times."

"I don't remember. I suppose . . . I wanted to scare them—the other two, I mean. Just scare them. So they'd go away."

Norah and Wyler looked at each other. Wyler would have liked to pursue the matter of the two companions. Norah didn't think Altman could tell them much more, not in her present state.

"Why don't you rest a while," Norah suggested. "Detective Wyler and I have some things to do. We'll be back later."

Stefanie Altman sighed with relief. "I am very tired. Thank you, Lieutenant Mulcahaney."

Wyler waited till they were outside in the hall and till he was sure the door was closed behind them. "There was no knife on the body."

"I know," Norah answered. "He could have dropped it when he fell. We have to make a thorough search."

Clarence Hurt lived one flight down. He answered his door as soon as Wyler rang.

"Is she all right?" he asked. "Should we call a doctor for her?"

Hurt was a professional pianist and occasional songwriter. That is, he wrote all the time but sold rarely. He performed in small, undistinguished supper clubs and cocktail lounges, usually in the suburbs. He was in his early forties. Heavy jowls and sagging belly testified to too many drinks through the long nights, bloodshot eyes to a lifetime in smoke-filled rooms. He would never make it to the top and he knew it, but he wasn't unhappy. In his tux, his working uniform, erect at the piano, Hurt still managed to look suave and summon up a certain distinction. At home, in cords and flannel shirt, unshaven, he was totally ordinary. It was his concern for his neighbor that distinguished him.

"Are you a close friend, Mr. Hurt?" Norah asked.

"I spend time in her bookstore. It's become a neighborhood hangout." He paused. "Yes," he decided. "I am a friend. She's got more friends than she knows."

"What exactly caused you to call 911 tonight?" Wyler asked.

"I was working on a new arrangement," he said, gesturing toward a small upright piano set in front of a small bay window. That and the hi-fi system were the only quality items in the room; everything else was mismatched and secondhand. "All of a sudden I heard voices down in the street. A woman yelled." He sighed. "This used to be a nice quiet neighborhood, but lately the drug dealers and the homeless . . . well, you try not to pay attention." He shrugged. "Then I heard a couple of shots. Something told me they were no backfire. Then there were more shouts and a couple more shots. I looked out the window and saw a woman kneeling over somebody on the sidewalk. When she raised her head I recognized Stefanie."

"That was when you called 911?" Wyler asked, and Hurt nodded. "Then what?"

"I got my coat and went down to see if I could help."

"And what did you find?"

"Stefanie was still kneeling over him and moaning over and over, 'I didn't mean to kill him. I didn't mean it.' "

"Did you look to see if he was, in fact, dead?" Norah put in quietly.

Clarence Hurt gasped. "No, ma'am. It never occurred to me. She was crying over him and there was a gun on the pavement beside her."

"Not in her hand?" Norah went on.

"No, she had a ski mask in her hand. God, I never thought to look and make sure."

"Don't be upset, Mr. Hurt. According to the medical examiner, he died instantly."

Hurt sighed.

"So you didn't actually see the shooting?" Wyler took over again. "You heard what sounded like an argument followed by the shots. Is that right?"

"Yes."

"How many shots were there?"

"First two, one after the other real fast. Then two more or maybe three, I'm not sure; quick, but not on top of each other like the first, if you get what I mean."

"Could it have been an exchange of fire?"

"Oh . . ." The witness shook his head. "I couldn't say."

"And how much of a lapse of time was there after the last shot till you looked out?"

"I waited till I was sure the shooting was over," Hurt admitted.

"And by then Ms. Altman was alone."

"Yes."

Wyler considered. He was looking for confirmation of Altman's claim that there had been three men. So he reviewed Hurt's statement once more. "You heard what sounded like an argument down on the street under your window. Then a woman screamed and there were two shots in rapid succession. A pause. More shouting and two or three more shots, not so rapid. Who was doing the shouting?"

"A woman and a man. The man yelled, 'You shot him; you shot him.' "

"When you went down and joined Ms. Altman, you saw the gun lying on the ground beside her and the ski mask in her hand. Was there anything else? Any other weapon in evidence? Another gun, or a knife maybe?"

Clarence Hurt shook his head. "No. I didn't see any other weapon."

Norah Mulcahaney and Simon Wyler stood at the top of the stoop and surveyed the snow-covered steps and pavement.

"We can't let it go till tomorrow," Norah said. She checked her watch; she could still make it to Brooklyn by subway. She'd be late for dinner, but it was Lena and Jake's company she wanted. "The snow's light; you can brush off the top layers. Pour boiling water over the rest. Franciscus and Weeks can get started. Once Tedesco and the others get here, it shouldn't take long. The search has priority. We've got to find that knife."

She scribbled her in-laws' number on a slip of paper. "Call me as soon as you've got it."

Wyler and his bucket brigade melted the snow on the stoop and the steps of the brownstone and all around the area where the body of Frank Beech had come to rest. No knife.

Next, the canvass of the neighborhood was organized. It took till midnight to cover those who were at home and answered the door and were willing to let the detectives inside. Results: inconclusive. Nobody admitted hearing the commotion on the stoop. Of those who reluctantly admitted hearing the shots, only a very few considered them to be anything other than a backfire and went to the window as Clarence Hurt had done. By then it was all over and of no use as evidence. A long night of futility, Wyler thought.

What came next was prescribed. Nevertheless, he did it reluctantly.

He returned to Altman's apartment and rang her bell. He had to ring several times before she answered. She was in robe and slippers. Her red, swollen eyes indicated she had cried herself to sleep. He felt even worse.

"I'm sorry to disturb you, Ms. Altman. I have to ask you to get dressed and come over to the station house with me."

"Now? Why?"

"We have to go over your testimony once more. We'll have to take your statement down and then you'll be asked to sign it."

"Can't it wait till morning?"

"I'm sorry."

A wave of nausea passed over Stefanie Altman. The lights seemed to dim and the floor under her feet to rock. She thought she was going to faint.

"Where's Lieutenant Mulcahaney? I want to speak to Lieutenant Mulcahaney."

"She's not available just now."

"She said she'd be back. She said she'd talk to me again."

"Later maybe, at the precinct."

"Three men threatened me! One of them pulled a knife. Don't you believe me? Doesn't anybody believe me?" Ste-

fanie Altman's large, myopic eyes bulged with despera-
tion.

"It doesn't matter whether I believe you, Ms. Altman,
or whether Lieutenant Mulcahaney believes you. The
facts are that a man is dead and you killed him."

CHAPTER
THREE

At 9:30 P.M. power to the subways failed. Lena and Jake wanted Norah to stay overnight, but she was uneasy about being cut off from the precinct. At eleven-thirty, it was announced that power had been restored and the subways were running again. Norah was relieved and headed for home.

When she awoke the next morning, the storm was over. A brilliant orange sunrise tinted the walls of her bedroom; by the time she got up and showered, it had changed to a cold white glare that reflected off the snow-covered roofs and the white, empty, silent streets. It would take a while for the city to get moving again, Norah thought, and took her time about dressing.

The phone rang just as she was sitting down to breakfast.

"Lieutenant? It's Fernando Arenas. Sorry to disturb you, but we have a homicide that requires your personal attention."

Ferdi Arenas was one of the original members of Norah's Senior Citizens squad, her first command when she made sergeant close to ten years ago. They had worked together ever since; they were friends. Yet in matters relating to the job Ferdi treated Norah with the full respect due a superior. In fact, Norah could gauge the gravity of a situation by the degree of Ferdi's formality. On that basis, and because he was calling her at home, Norah assumed that this was big.

"The complaint comes from a Mrs. Armanda Sequi at the Belgrave on Central Park West. The victim is Mrs. Gilda Valente."

Norah caught her breath. The name Valente was well known to the public and the police, but had there been any doubt as to which Valente this was, the address was familiar to every law enforcement officer in the city—to the DEA (Drug Enforcement Administration), Organized Crime Force, Prostitution Squad, Narcotics . . . name it.

"Details?" Norah asked.

"She was drowned."

"Drowned?"

"They have an enclosed swimming pool on the roof."

What else? Norah thought. "I'll take the subway and meet you there."

Despite the brilliant sunshine, it was bitter cold. Norah didn't even want to know what the windchill factor might be. She pulled the wool scarf up over her nose and pulled the wool cap down to her eyebrows and left the comparative shelter of her doorway. Porters were just starting to clear single-file paths in front of their buildings. On Lexington Avenue a single snowplow labored. It would be midafternoon at best before any of the side streets could be made passable for traffic even here in mid-Manhattan. She wouldn't even hazard a guess as to the boroughs. For once, the weather forecast had been right.

Norah came out of the subway at the Museum of Natural History and walked uptown to the elegant Art Deco building with its twin towers. A couple of RMPs were parked as close to the curb as the snow permitted, but the usual row of official cars that routinely turned out for a homicide had not arrived. Not Forensics and, as far as Norah could tell, nobody from the DA nor the Medical Examiner's offices either. The last two might, like her, be coming by public transportation, but one way or another they'd turn up. In fact, Norah expected the best and brightest of the ADAs and the chief ME himself, Phillip Worgan. It wouldn't surprise her if someone from the Big Building came—Inspector Felix or even Chief of Detectives Luis Deland. As she approached the building entrance, she noted that the sidewalk along the entire block had been shoveled clear and a uniformed doorman was on duty outside.

She flashed her shield case.

"Yes, ma'am." He opened the door for her. "There's a private elevator to the penthouse down that way."

The heat enveloped Norah like an electric blanket as she crossed the marble lobby and turned the corner. Two linebacker types stepped in her path.

"Lieutenant Mulcahaney, Homicide." Again she displayed her open shield case. "Do you work for the building or for Mr. Valente?"

"Mr. Valente."

"This is your regular post?"

"Yes, ma'am."

"What time did you come on?"

"Seven A.M."

They were well spoken, Norah thought, and well groomed. Slick in their three-piece suits, they could almost pass for FBI.

"That's your regular schedule?" They nodded. "And everything was normal when you came on? The team you relieved didn't report any problem?" No need to ask if there was another team; Dario Valente would surely have guards on duty around the clock.

"No, ma'am."

"You didn't report at the penthouse?"

"We never go up unless Mr. Valente sends for us, or Mrs. Valente."

Norah noticed a wall phone. "Is that a direct line to the apartment?"

"Yes, ma'am."

"All right. Thank you. I'll go up now."

They separated so she could pass. The spokesman produced a key, released the single button on the panel, and stepped out of the elevator. Double protection, Norah thought as the doors closed smoothly and the car rose to the accompaniment of the strains of the overture to *Rosenkavalier.*

Obviously a regular button panel was unnecessary since the car was not intended to make intervening stops. But there was a floor indicator overhead to help maintain orientation, and Norah watched the numbers flash to twenty-one, then to PH. The car stopped and the door opened. She stepped out into a small, plain vestibule done in twenties style—silver wallpaper and a single door in black lacquer. She rang.

The door was opened by a dark, slender young man. Although not as physically intimidating as the two downstairs, he was of the same category, perhaps even a cut above. His suit was a little more expensive, his hair a little better groomed, more handsome. His face was narrow, sallow, set in grave concern.

"I'm Mr. Valente's personal secretary, Salvatore Nunzio." He pronounced *Salvatore* sounding the final vowel in the Italian way.

Norah nodded. "I'd like to see Mr. Valente."

"He's not at home, Lieutenant. He's at his country place. We're trying to reach him. Meantime, if there's anything I can do for you, anything you need . . ."

He was excessively polite and usually Norah didn't like that, but Nunzio seemed genuinely anxious to help. "Thank you, I'll want to talk to you later. Now if you'll show me . . ."

"The pool. Of course. This way."

He led Norah through a spacious living room, very modern, almost austere, yet suggesting a degree of opulence she'd never encountered before. A scent of roses and gardenias wafted from beyond an open sliding glass door; the pool terrace. Norah had already unwound her muffler and now she pulled off her storm coat. About to step over the coaming, she paused to study a photograph in a silver frame on a crystal side table. It was an eight-by-ten black-

and-white glossy of a young woman in evening dress. Her face was a perfect oval, her brow high and clear, her eyes large and luminous, her dark hair coiled around her head. The gown was heavy satin, its bodice encrusted with glittering stones and pearls. She held herself like a princess. The picture was familiar. Copies of it had illustrated the programs of countless society affairs, had accompanied newspaper and magazine articles. Its subject had instant public recognition equal to that of the most glamorous of movie stars.

Salvatore Nunzio cleared his throat. "I'll be in my office, Lieutenant, second door to the right." He indicated it and backed off.

Stepping over the threshold, Norah entered an oasis of summer in the midst of the snow. The pool was of Olympic proportions, its blue waters sparkling in the sun that flooded through the transparent, retractable dome. Trees, shrubs, and flowers in redwood tubs turned it into a bower. Wrought-iron furniture with bright cushions invited lounging. At the center of it all, floating lazily in the scintillating water, dark hair spread around her head—the victim. Facedown. Nude.

As Norah walked over, Sergeant Fernando Arenas met her. He was ten years younger but he looked older. His black hair was prematurely laced with gray and receding. The lines around his eyes and at the corner of his mouth were outer remnants of the despair he had experienced at the death of his fiancée, Pilar Nieves. Pilar, a police officer also, had been on decoy duty with Ferdi as her backup. She had been ambushed and knifed before his very eyes and had died in his arms. Norah had patiently reviewed every facet of the tragedy to show him he wasn't to blame. She had mourned with him and then helped him to pick up his life again. Nevertheless, it had taken Fernando Arenas five years to find inner peace, five years before he so much as looked at another woman. Norah had been the matron of honor when he married Concepción. Now, he was the father of twin girls. Concepción was pregnant again and due to give birth in a couple of weeks.

The two of them stood side by side looking at the nude body in the middle of the pool.

"Who found her?"

"The aunt, Mrs. Armanda Sequi."

"Like this?"

"As you see her," he replied quietly. Ferdi had been thin and nervous till his marriage. In the two years since he had filled out to 145 pounds of contentment and developed a calm demeanor that was a steadying influence on those around him.

For several moments neither Norah nor Arenas moved as they continued to survey the golden-brown body. No bathing-suit marks spoiled the evenness of her tan. She was in every way perfect, Norah thought: about five four, slender, buttocks rounded, legs tapering in a firm line from thighs to narrow ankles, arms spread out as though she was in the midst of a breaststroke. Both knew that formal identification required her to be turned faceup, but that would have to wait till a photographic record was made of the scene and the medical examiner arrived.

"What time did Mrs. Sequi find her?" Norah asked.

"She came upstairs at seven A.M."

"This is a duplex?"

"No. Mrs. Sequi lives in the building in her own apartment. She's taken care of Mrs. Valente since Mrs. Valente was a young girl. She came over with her when the marriage was arranged. She more or less runs the household for Mrs. Valente."

"I see. What other staff is there?"

"The secretary, you just met him; cook, chauffeur. They also have quarters in the building. Bodyguards and two daily maids come from outside."

"In essence there's no live-in staff," Norah concluded. "How about security?"

"Round the clock downstairs at the private elevator. The service entrance is closed and locked at six P.M. for the entire building."

"And Valente's supposed to be at his country house. Where's that?"

"Bucks County," Ferdi replied. "The storm hit real hard there. Power lines are down and service won't be restored for at least another twenty-four hours. That includes telephone."

Norah took a deep breath, held it, and slowly released it. Dario Valente, a *capo* of one of the most powerful Mafia families in the East, was known to be deeply in love with his young wife. His reaction to her murder would be a big factor in the investigation. Valente could hinder or help. He had power. How would he use it? The hubbub accompanying the arrival of the technical crew and the ME with his people interrupted her speculation.

As she had anticipated, Phillip Worgan himself had answered the call; this was not a case for second-stringers. She herself would probably be superseded soon enough, Norah thought. Meantime, the case belonged to the Fourth Zone—to Ferdi and to her.

The photographers set up. Fingerprints wanted to know what the lieut was particularly interested in.

"I'm not sure yet. I guess you can't lift anything off the metal armrests."

Worgan strolled over to stand beside Norah at the edge of the pool and looked out at the body.

"I suppose it is Gilda Valente?"

"Her aunt says so. She found her."

"This is going to shake a lot of people."

"I know."

"I take it Valente isn't here. Has he been notified?"

"He's at his place in the country. The telephone lines are down."

Phillip Worgan looked at Norah searchingly from behind tinted, aviator-style glasses. At thirty-two, Worgan was young to be Chief Medical Examiner for the City of New York. Medium height, with thick brown hair and bushy eyebrows, his bony shoulders stooping under the weight of the old, worn Burberry overcoat, he didn't present a particularly prepossessing appearance. Having come from Syracuse, where he'd been in charge, he had joined the New York City office as an assistant, displaying the arrogant assurance that he would, upon the retirement of the incumbent, the legendary Asa Osterman, fill the same post here. But though his medical credentials were exceptional, Phil Worgan discovered that more was required for acceptance and much more for success. Tact, for one thing. His manner in the early times triggered resentment that solidified into a wall between him and the police in particular. Norah Mulcahaney had been one of the few officers who had not tried to undercut him. He was grateful. He cared about her and wanted to be sure she didn't ignore the political aspects of this case. Dario Valente's influence radiated in many directions, reached down into the substrata of crime and up to the seats of power.

"We can't wait," he told her.

And Norah knew very well that Worgan's appointment to chief remained subject to challenge at least till the end of the year when his tenure would be confirmed, so the situation was sensitive for him too.

"No reason we should."

Their eyes met. Then Worgan indicated the body of the victim in the pool. "I'm not anxious to swim out to her."

Norah grinned.

A skimmer, a long pole with a net at the end intended to clear debris from the water surface, was located in a maintenance closet and served to maneuver the body gently to the side where the morgue attendants could reach her and lift her out. In that process, all other work stopped. Everyone there was a pro, accustomed to death in various guises—in ugliness, violence, sorrow—yet they drew near to watch as the golden figure was laid on the terrazzo floor and turned over. The promise was fulfilled. She was slim and at the same time voluptuous; her breasts were full; her waist narrow; thighs generous; the dark triangle of pubic hair glinting with threads of gold. She would have been a thing of beauty but for the contortion of her face and eyes that were open in horror.

With a soft, collective sigh, the men went back to work. Kneeling at her side, Phillip Worgan first leaned out and put his hand into the water. "Anybody check the thermostat?"

"Seventy-two, Doc," Arenas replied.

Worgan now proceeded with the examination. He was quick and thorough. "It appears the cause of death was drowning," he told Norah. "I find no bruises or contusions. Certain questions do arise, however. I'm sure they've occurred to you. I'll have to check the lungs, for one thing, and do blood tests. The usual."

Norah nodded.

"It would help to know when she took her last meal. Also her habits regarding the use of the pool."

Norah looked around once more. Except for a single eight-ounce glass and the dregs of whatever it had contained—might be Coke—and for a blue-and-green-striped beach towel that was still damp and draped across the foot of a chaise, everything appeared in perfect order, ash trays clean, pillows precisely plumped, terrazzo floor mopped and polished. It would seem either the pool wasn't used much or the housekeeping was faultless. She ordered the glass and the towel to be sent for lab testing.

"Unless you need more pictures, we'll take her," Worgan concluded.

Norah stood by and watched while Gilda Valente, droplets of water still shimmering on her tawny skin, was placed in the body bag, the zipper closed, and the straps secured.

"Where's the aunt?" she asked Ferdi.

They found Armanda Sequi alone in the pantry, eyes red from crying but, for the moment anyway, calm.

"I'm very sorry to intrude at this time, Mrs. Sequi," Norah said, "but there are certain questions we must ask."

The aunt nodded, wiped her eyes with a grubby handkerchief. She was a stolid country woman of about fifty. In her plain, traditional black dress, her iron-gray hair pulled back uncompromisingly into a tight knot, she reminded Norah of her mother-in-law, although Signora Emilia was at least thirty years older. These women clung to the customs of the old country, Norah thought, regardless of age.

"How long have you been in America, Mrs. Sequi?" Norah asked, partly to put the witness at ease as much as possible and partly because she sensed it would be important later on.

"Six years. I was with Gilda when she came as a bride. I raised the child. Her parents were killed in an accident, a car accident. Gilda was fifteen. There was no other family, so I took her in."

Though she spoke with a marked accent, she spoke fluently and correctly, Norah noted. It also seemed to her that Mrs. Sequi had lightly stressed the word *accident*.

"She was like a daughter to me." The woman's eyes brimmed. "Dario knew this. He also understood that Gilda would feel strange in her new life, so he brought me over with her. He is a good man."

The tears quivered in her eyes and threatened to spill over, but her peasant pride would not permit a breakdown before strangers. Armanda Sequi wiped her eyes angrily with a gesture that seemed to say she would not allow anything, even grief, to get in the way of avenging her niece.

"What do you want to know?"

"Everything that happened this morning, beginning with when you got up," Norah replied.

"I got up at six as usual. I dressed and made myself breakfast. Then I came upstairs. It was seven."

"Did you have to take the regular elevator from your apartment down to the lobby first?"

"No, no. I use the service elevator. It is closed from eight to six, but I have a key that permits me to use it at any time."

"I assume that while it's in use there's a guard."

"Yes. He calls on the telephone to make sure the delivery is . . . legitimate."

"I see. Go on."

"I am always the first one up here. I walk through the apartment, open the curtains, clean up—ash trays, dirty glasses—so that if Dario or Gilda come out before the maids the place looks . . ." Again she searched for the appropriate word and settled for— "nice. Dario and Gilda are both early risers."

"And this morning?"

"I knew Dario was not at home. He had called Gilda yesterday to say he would stay in the country one more night because of the storm. She told me to inform the cook not to bother about dinner, just to leave her something cold in the refrigerator."

"What time was this?"

"About five. Just before I went down to my own place."

"Is that when you usually go?"

"Yes. Unless Gilda is planning to attend the opera or one of her society affairs. Then I stay to help her dress."

"But last night she didn't ask you to stay?" Armanda Sequi shook her head. "So you went down to . . . what floor are you on, Mrs. Sequi?"

"The eighteenth."

"Using the service elevator with your special key."

"Yes."

"Who else has a key?"

"The guards and Salvatore, Mr. Valente's secretary."

"All right, you went down to your own apartment at a little after five. Then what did you do? Were you at home all evening?"

"No, I went to the house of my friend, Giustina di Lucca, in the Bronx."

"In spite of the storm?"

"I took the subway."

"How did you get back? The subways were out for several hours."

"I waited till they started again. I was home by twelve-thirty."

"Did you come up here?"

"No." Her still-reddened eyes flickered. "I had no reason."

"So the last time you saw Gilda Valente was here at approximately five yesterday afternoon."

"It was in her sitting room," Mrs. Sequi corrected. "It is a combination parlor and office."

Norah nodded. "And when you left, was Salvatore Nunzio still in the apartment?"

"I don't know. You will have to ask him."

"All right, let's get back to this morning. You came up in the service elevator. You entered . . . ?"

"Through the back." She indicated the far end of the big, sunny, old-fashioned pantry in which they sat, and an open door that led to a very modern, gleaming white and aluminum kitchen. From what Norah glimpsed it could serve a small restaurant.

"So you started your inspection passing from the kitchen, through here, then into the dining room. From the dining room you entered the main hall and then the living room." Now they were getting to the hard part, Norah thought, but the stolid face remained graven.

"Was there anything in the living room that had to be cleared—drinks, ash trays, newspapers?"

"I don't know. I didn't look. The first thing I saw was that the drapes were open and the pool lights on. It was unusual. I went over to the light panel and I saw her—Gilda." She had to stop then. She had to clamp her jaw tight to hold back the sobs that were throbbing in her throat, forming knots, choking her. "For one second, I thought she was having an early-morning swim. She did that sometimes. I told myself she was doing it again. But I knew that I was deluding myself, that something terrible had happened. She wasn't swimming. She was facedown in the water and she wasn't moving. *Santa Maria, Madre di Dio,* she wasn't moving."

The sobs erupted. "How could such a thing happen?" she demanded. "It is not possible. Gilda was a fine swimmer. Dario, he had the pool installed for her pleasure. How could it happen?" she pleaded between great, gasping sobs.

Ferdi Arenas went into the kitchen and got her a glass of water. Her hand shook violently so that she spilled most of it but she did manage to swallow some and when she was finished, she was calmer.

"What happened next, Mrs. Sequi? What did you do?" Norah asked.

"I called Dario."

"Before 911?"

"Certainly. It was his right to be informed."

"You knew where to reach him?"

"At the house, of course." The look she flashed at Norah was one of impatience, even annoyance. "He had been there five days and he called to say he would stay one more night. I told you that. But I couldn't get through. The operator said the lines were down because of the storm."

"All right, Mrs. Sequi. Now I have to ask you a very important question. You were like a mother to Gilda Valente. You were with her at a very critical time in her life and then you came here to live with her and her husband. You have been a part of the household since the beginning. Would you say it was a happy marriage? Did Mr. and Mrs. Valente get along?"

The grief was set aside and for a moment her ravaged face almost glowed. "He worshiped the ground she walked on."

"She was much younger than he, wasn't she?"

"It is not unusual for a man of Dario Valente's importance to take a young wife. It is to ensure many sons." The realization overwhelmed her with a new wave of pain and regret: There were no sons and now there never would be.

CHAPTER FOUR

There was no indication of a break-in, and unauthorized access to the penthouse seemed all but impossible. Norah instituted a search anyway. With Salvatore Nunzio as guide, she and Arenas made a tour of the premises and were more impressed at each step with the style in which the Valentes lived. Certainly, there was plenty around to steal—an esoteric collection of art works, a splendor of jewelry carelessly jumbled in an unlocked antique box on Gilda Valente's dressing table. Nothing appeared to be missing, according to Nunzio.

"There is, of course, the insurance company's list of all the paintings and sculptures as well as of Mrs. Valente's jewelry," the secretary told Norah. "I have a copy in the files if you'd care to see it."

"Thank you."

In the study that served as Dario Valente's office, Nunzio showed them the safe but, trusted though he was, he didn't have access to that. It showed no indication of tampering, however. Who would dare to steal from the *capo?*

While Norah continued to look around, Arenas put some questions to Nunzio in a seemingly casual way. "What time did you leave last night?"

"Five-thirty." Answered without hesitation.

"At the same time as Mrs. Sequi."

"We do usually both leave around then, but not together. Yesterday she used the rear elevator and I went
down through the front lobby."

Norah came over. "I thought you lived in the building."

"I do. Last night was my poker night. The game was
down in the Village. I thought, in view of the weather, I'd
better get an early start."

"How about the others in the game? Did everybody
make it?"

"Yes, Lieutenant. I can give you a list of names and addresses."

"That would be helpful. What time did the game break
up?"

"A little after two. The subways were slow, so I didn't
get back till three."

"You didn't get much sleep," Norah observed. "I assume you were awakened."

"At seven. Or a little after. Armanda, Mrs. Sequi, called
me."

"What exactly did she say?"

"That I was needed upstairs right away."

"Nothing else?"

He shook his head.

"And when you came up, where was she?"

"Still at the pool. She didn't want to leave Mrs. Valente
alone. I insisted, but she wouldn't go, not till the sergeant
arrived." Nunzio indicated Arenas.

When Norah and Ferdi finally left the penthouse, one
question haunted Norah: How would Dario Valente, head
of the powerful Canonico Family, react when he found
out about the death of his beautiful young wife? What
would he do?

As they plodded back to the station house, it occurred
to Norah that it would be some time till Dario Valente
found out. Snowbound in the Bucks County, the power
lines down and resumption of telephone service at best a
couple of days off as crews went about the job of restoring
connections on an individual basis, it could be days before
he found out. Unless he had a transistor radio. Usually

the name of a murder victim was withheld pending notification of the family. In this instance, Norah doubted the compassionate practice would be observed.

In recent months, Mafia power had been gravely, even fatally weakened. Ties to organized labor were undermined by new interpretation of an old statute, RICO (Racketeer Influence and Corrupt Organizations Act), passed in 1970 that permitted seizure of assets and FBI infiltration, and offered witnesses long-term protection. Brought to the bar of justice in the "Commission" case, three *capo*s of leading *Cosa Nostra* families were convicted and sentenced to terms of one hundred years each. Unprecedented. Not long after, the United States attorney for the southern district brought the "Pizza Connection" trial to a successful conclusion. Two of the Mafia's top bosses and sixteen others were found guilty in a $1.6 billion drug smuggling scheme. The removal of these key men left the organization in the hands of inexperienced bosses so that control of such unions as teamsters, restaurant, hotel, construction, shipping, and countless others was seriously affected. Dario Valente, whose star had been rising long before the spate of convictions, was now destined for the height of the firmament of organized crime. Yet Norah could not wish even such a man the shock of hearing about the death of the woman he loved over the radio.

Having been married to an Italian, Norah understood the emotional currents that motivated them. She also had experience with the arrogance of power, and combining the two, she thought she knew what to expect from Dario Valente. He would want to get back and take charge. He would want to throw his own people into the investigation. She sighed inwardly; that was something the brass would have to deal with.

In fact, Norah was surprised that during the hours at the Valente residence, none of the top guns of the department or the DA's office had put in an appearance. Maybe it was because of the snow; the streets were still clogged and VIPs were not inclined to use public transportation—

not without a photographer to document the journey. It could also be that by not coming they were indicating the Valente case was not to be given exaggerated importance; that it would receive the same attention as, neither more nor less than, any other homicide. So the case was theirs, Norah thought as she and Arenas entered the station house—at least until Dario Valente returned.

When would that be? she wondered. He could fly in. There were several small airports catering to private planes and commuter helicopters in Bucks County. But it would take another twenty-four hours for the roads to be cleared so he could drive to such an airport. Maybe more.

Norah was wrong on two counts.

Dario Valente was alone in the Retreat, a small colonial set on forty-seven acres of rolling hills and fertile farmland. The house dated from 1800 and had been restored with love and integrity. There were chestnut and pine plank floors, four fireplaces, and cherry paneling in the main room. Above all, there was solitude. Early in the marriage, Valente discovered that Gilda didn't like the seclusion that was such a solace for him, so he stopped bringing her along. Gilda was a hothouse creature. She required a support team of domestics, whereas he intended this to be his private world. He came to hike, hunt, ride. Very rarely to conduct business. He brought no staff, not even his personal secretary; no guards. Out here, he could fend for himself.

Dario Valente was forty-eight, an imposing six foot three, a fit 205 pounds. He had a broad, dark face, wide shoulders, and a barrel chest. At the age when most men's hair started thinning and graying, his swept back from a high brow thick and jet black. He was a powerful man and he exuded power; even a stranger unfamiliar with his history would sense it. As he sat alone on the snowy night, feet propped up on a rough oak coffee table he had built himself, in the light and warmth of the blazing fire, which he fed with logs cut from his own trees, Valente was enjoying the Lenore Overture No. 3 on his newly installed stereo. At eleven-forty precisely, the power went off. He had not turned on any lights so he was aware of it only because the music stopped. Halted, would be more accurate, for within seconds, the private, backup generator clicked on reassuringly and the music resumed. Dario Valente was a provident man. He had stacked plenty of firewood beside the hearth, enough for warmth and light should the backup fail. With the storm raging around him, he could let himself slip into deep slumber.

He woke once at a little after 2:00 A.M. He noted the snow was still falling, banked the fire, and went up to his second-floor bedroom where he fell instantly asleep again.

He slept late and awoke to a warm house and outside a brilliant sun shining on the kind of country scene city people rarely see except on Christmas cards. He was both dazzled and dismayed. The snow had leveled road, fields, hills into one vast white expanse. The driveway was under at least two feet. He had a small snow blower in the garage but it wouldn't be adequate to the job even if he could get it out. Not that it mattered. It was a long meandering road to the front gate, and assuming he could clear the way for his car to reach the gate he would be blocked there till the town plows came through. One of these days he should have a small helicopter pad constructed, Valente thought. It would mean bulldozing some of his cherished oaks and breaching his privacy in the process. He might as well get rid of the place as do that.

He dressed slowly to savor the extra dimension of tranquillity brought on by the total isolation. But he found it oppressive. Not bothering to shave, still in slippers, Valente went downstairs to fix himself some breakfast. He turned on the radio—loud. He was having his second cup of black, Medaglia d'Oro coffee and his first cigarette when the news bulletin announced Gilda's death.

He broke out into an icy sweat. From healthy outdoor ruddiness, his color went to ash. The announcement had been brief, had stated merely that Gilda Valente, wife of Dario Valente, powerful *capo* of the Canonico Family, had been found dead that morning in the pool of their luxurious penthouse. Nothing more. No indication of whether it was regarded as an accident or foul play.

A vision of Gilda as he had first seen her in the church of Santa Caterina in the dusty Sicilian village where they both had their roots flashed before him. It was a vision against which he had matched every other woman since. It was the day after the funeral of her parents. She had been alone, kneeling in front of the statue of the saint, the tiny flames of votive candles illuminating her grave young face. Right then, he had fallen in love. Right then, he had determined to marry her.

With a shaking hand, Valente ground out the cigarette and went to the kitchen wall phone and picked up the receiver. No dial tone. He jiggled the hook. Nothing. Naturally the lines were down. What should he do? He had to do something. He was normally a controlled man, a patient man. He found, to his own dismay, that the need to take action was overwhelming. What could he do? His people must be trying to reach him, and the police too, of course, but until power was restored and the roads open, they were as helpless as he was. He lit another cigarette. There was nothing anyone could do but wait.

No, he thought. Wrong.

He ground out the barely started cigarette on the edge of the plate with what was left of the fried eggs and, careful housekeeper that he was when on his own, didn't even bother to stack the dirty dishes in the sink.

Upstairs, he made his preparations quickly and efficiently. He changed clothes from the skin out, putting on long johns, then layering undershirt, shirt, sweater, thin nylon parka. He chose waterproof lumberman's boots and laced them to midcalf. He pulled on a knitted cap that could be rolled down as a mask against the cold. He packed a knapsack with a couple of sandwiches, a chocolate bar, a thermos of hot coffee. He shut the front door behind him and started out.

It was just after 10:00 A.M. The sun on the snow was blindingly bright. The snow was light, fluffy, easily displaced, nevertheless it was over his knees in most places so that walking was a heavy exertion. At this rate it would be midafternoon before he reached his destination, Valente thought. He might as well turn back. All this effort would gain him half a day at best. At worst, he might make it to the small, private airport only to find no plane available. If he turned back to the house, he might find that phone service had been restored and he could order a private plow to come through and get him. Nevertheless, even as he called up reasons to turn back, Dario Valente kept moving forward.

He peeled off first his parka, then the sweater. By three in the afternoon the sun was low in the west, the shadows lengthening; the wind had picked up, and his sweat was freezing on him. He put on the clothing he had taken off. In the shelter of a small grove of pines marking the juncture of two secondary roads, he stopped to rest and eat. The food and coffee warmed him a little, but the warmth didn't last. His arms and legs were too tired to keep up the pace necessary to stay warm.

By four-thirty it was nearly dark and Valente had not seen a single person. He was barely moving. With the help of a rising moon and his familiarity with the landscape he was able to maintain his course. Ahead, at what in his weakened condition appeared an interminable distance, he thought he recognized the lights of the airfield. Between him and those lights, he could make out a few houses, modest homes he'd never noticed from behind the windows of his limousine. Suppose he went up to one of them and rang the bell? Surely they would let him in to rest. A half hour or so and he could go on. But in his heart, Dario Valente knew that once he entered into warmth and comfort, if he so much as sat down in a chair, he would not get up again. At 7:35 P.M. in deep night darkness, nearly ten hours since he'd set out, Valente reached the door of the Inter County Air Service office shack and stumbled inside.

Harry Babcock, owner and chief pilot, looked up, surprise turning to shock. "My God, Mr. Valente, is that you?"

"I have to get to New York right away."

"We're shut down, Mr. Valente. You can see for yourself; we can't get off the ground."

Norah Mulcahaney had misjudged the *capo*'s will and she had also misread her own position. The call wakened her from a sound sleep.

"Jim Felix, Norah."

According to the radium digital readout of her bedroom clock it was 1:01 A.M. Inspector James Felix was Chief of Detectives Luis Deland's right-hand man. He was also Norah's friend. Not sure under which guise he was making the call, she answered formally. "Yes, sir."

"Sorry to disturb you, Norah, but I just had a call from the chief. He had a call from Dario Valente."

She pulled herself up a little straighter. So, it had happened sooner than anticipated. They'd fixed the telephone lines over there in Pennsylvania and Valente had got right on and was throwing his weight around, demanding high-quality, personal attention. But why should Jim Felix call her at this hour to tell her she was off the case? Couldn't it have waited till morning?

"He wants to talk to you," Felix told her. "Valente, not the chief."

"Me?"

"I told him Sergeant Arenas is carrying the case and you're in command of the squad. That's right, isn't it?"

He knew it was. Norah swung her legs over the side of the bed, ready for anything. "Yes, sir."

"Okay, so he's waiting for you. Get there as fast as you can."

"Yes, sir." Norah paused. It would be a hell of a trip. "It depends on the condition of the roads," she pointed out.

"Where do you think you're going? He's back. In New York. At the penthouse."

"Already? I didn't expect the roads would be cleared for another twelve hours, probably more."

"They're not. He walked. It took him almost ten hours to get to the airport and it was closed. He demanded and got men from the town to shovel a runway so he could take off. He landed at the downtown heliport. Got a taxi to take him to the morgue where he viewed his wife. After that, he went home. He's suffering from prolonged exposure and hypothermia. He wants to see you and talk to you. He refuses medication until he does."

Norah jumped to her feet. "I'm on my way." She had an afterthought. "Will I meet you there?"

"Do you need me?"

"No, sir."

"I didn't think so."

Another pair of young men interchangeable with the two she'd seen on her previous visit stood guard at the penthouse elevator. The night shift. As soon as she displayed her shield, they sprang to serve her. When she reached the penthouse, Sal Nunzio was in the vestibule waiting to usher her inside.

"Thank you for coming, Lieutenant."

The secretary's tone was hushed. He reminded Norah of those gravely sympathetic young men that met one at the doors of funeral parlors. He led her past the darkened living room without so much as a glance toward the also-darkened pool terrace, directly to the bedroom wing. He knocked lightly at the door of the master suite and yet another of Valente's retinue respectfully admitted them. He seemed to have an inexhaustible supply of these personable young men eager to serve him and to be a part of his organization. It was a big jump up, much higher than twenty-one stories, from the slums to this.

Dario Valente lay in the center of a magnificent four-poster propped up by pillows. The man had forced himself to exhaustion, had driven himself to the limit of endurance and beyond, yet he was a dominating presence. His left eye was swollen nearly shut and the massive discoloration extended down to his jaw. On the right side, his hand-some, rugged face was cut and scraped. He was flushed with fever. A spasm jerked through his body and he had to wait for it to pass before he could speak. Then his voice, though low, was firm.

"Lieutenant Mulcahaney. I'm sorry to bring you out at this hour."

Instantly, the young man who had admitted them placed a chair for Norah at the bedside. Another, almost as young, whom she now identified by his medical bag, snapped it shut.

"Don't let him tire himself," the doctor warned Norah. "If you need me, Mr. Valente, I'll be right outside."

The *capo* waited till he was gone and the door was firmly closed.

"You already know my secretary, and this is my chauffeur, Paolo Fiori. You don't mind if they stay? They are my close associates. I trust them and I want them to be fully conversant with the progress of the investigation into my wife's death."

"As you wish."

"Thank you. I am familiar with your record, Lieutenant Mulcahaney, and I feel that you have both the skill and experience and the compassion necessary to find out what happened. I am content to have you in charge."

Presumably he meant it as a compliment, but Norah felt patronized. It was hard to remember that this fine-looking man, who despite his condition was making every effort to show her courtesy and consideration, was a leading crime figure, responsible for countless murders and trafficking in human pain. That this man, who underlined the need for a woman's compassion toward the death of another woman, debased women through drugs and prostitution.

"Have you formed an opinion regarding my wife's death?"

"It's very early in the investigation, Mr. Valente."

"All right. Yes. But surely you have some . . . instinct?"

"We don't operate on instinct, Mr. Valente."

"Of course not." He paused and sought another approach. "Do you believe it might have been an accident?"

"I'm told your wife was an excellent swimmer."

"Absolutely. She used the pool on a regular basis for fitness and she also used it to enjoy herself."

"Were there set times at which she used the pool?"

"She swam laps in the morning on a regular basis. She might swim again at any time of the day or night."

Norah cast a glance at the two young men, the secretary and the chauffeur. "Naked?"

"The pool is strictly private," Valente told her.

"Was Mrs. Valente taking any kind of medication? Anything that might have made her drowsy, slowed her reflexes?"

"No."

"I must say an accident appears unlikely," Norah admitted, "but then so does a break-in. Your security is very good. There are no signs of an intruder. The initial medical examination has revealed no marks or bruises on the victim."

He smiled. "All right, Lieutenant, you've made your point."

"Thank you. I'd be glad to hear your ideas."

He sighed. "I have enemies. Many enemies."

"I understand that in your code retaliation, or vengeance if you prefer, isn't visited on the wife or children."

"Unfortunately, there are persons for whom the code no longer has significance."

Norah looked directly into the *capo*'s eyes. "Who hated you enough to kill your wife?"

Valente's lips closed into a hard line; his eyes narrowed and nearly shut. He shook his head. "Not yet."

Norah nodded; he was giving back some of her own.

"So, Lieutenant Mulcahaney, you will have all my cooperation in your investigation. I could put my own people on it . . ." He held up a hand as Norah started to speak. "I said *could*. I will not interfere with you; that's a promise. But while you are proceeding, Salvatore and Paolo will be asking questions of their counterparts in other organizations. You don't mind, Lieutenant?"

She hesitated, then decided to be honest. "Would it matter?"

He regarded her steadily, more closely than at any time since she'd sat down beside his bed. "No," he replied finally. "As I said, I could put my own people on this and neither you nor any of your bosses, go as high as you like, could stop it. So let's agree on this: Salvatore and Paolo will ask their questions discreetly. What they find out, if pertinent, will be passed on to you."

"You are to determine the pertinence or lack of it?"

"Of course."

Nonnegotiable, Norah thought. Valente made no pretense of being other than he was; he neither flaunted nor downplayed the power he wielded. She couldn't respect him, but she was nevertheless impressed. However, she had to extract certain assurances. "You won't act on the information yourself? You will allow us, the police, to investigate whatever clues are turned? And finally, when we apprehend the perpetrator, you will not interfere with due process."

"Due process—that's what I want."

"All right, Mr. Valente, we have a deal."

She didn't offer her hand and she hoped he wouldn't offer his. Being sensitive enough to know she wouldn't take it, he didn't.

Norah went on. "It would help if you could tell me about last night. You had planned to return to the city. Why did you change your mind?"

But the *capo* had reached his limit. With a gasp that was almost a rattle in his throat, Dario Valente slumped sideways on the pillows, eyes closed, chest heaving as he fought for breath.

"Get the doctor," Norah told Nunzio.

In seconds the doctor was there, hypodermic syringe in hand. After the injection, they all waited. Gradually, the breathing became less stertorous and finally returned to normal.

The young men were relieved.

"The interview is over," the physician told Norah.

Salvatore Nunzio placed himself at Norah's shoulder to see her out.

"Lieutenant," Valente called weakly but clearly. "Find out how my Gilda died. Solve the case so I can put vengeance aside. So I can mourn."

In the lobby, Valente's two guards were holding a television crew at bay. But they were only two and, as the elevator doors opened and Norah Mulcahaney stepped out, the pack closed around her. Someone thrust a microphone at her.

"Lieutenant, does your presence here mean that Gilda Valente's death was not an accident?"

"No comment."

"How is Dario Valente? Has he been seriously affected by the ordeal?"

"You'll have to ask his doctor," Norah said, and with the help of the guards made it to the main corridor.

"Lieutenant Mulcahaney!"

The voice wasn't loud, yet it was clearly audible over the noise and confusion. It had authority. Recognizing that, Norah turned and looked into amber eyes that steadily regarded her. Peripherally, she became aware of a square, rugged face—call it ugly or handsome, but nothing in between, she thought. The rest of him was unremarkable. He was dressed like everybody else—in loose, rough clothes suitable to the weather. Nevertheless, those who had pressed in on her now fell back to make way, deferring to him.

"Lieutenant Mulcahaney, what got you over here at one-forty-five A.M.?" he asked, and held up the microphone confidently expecting a reply.

The question was shrewd and very much to the point. "A.M. or P.M., it doesn't matter. I don't keep office hours."

"Come on, Lieutenant, you don't get out of bed in the middle of the night for no reason," the reporter insisted, but he was smiling as though they shared a special bond.

"Gilda Valente's body was discovered early this morning—that is to say, yesterday morning. You were here then. What brings you back?"

Norah frowned. Did she know him? He acted like it. And he did look familiar. Suddenly, she was aware of silence as the rest of the group waited for her answer. Then she had it. She knew who this was: Randall Tye, of course. Randall Tye, one of the anchors for the new Liberty Network News. Randall Tye was just coming into nationwide prominence but he was important enough not to have to chase down his own stories, Norah thought. He had leg men for that. He could sit at his desk and have the news handed to him for approval, to use or to be discarded. A gleam brightened Norah's dark blue eyes. She raised her chin.

"What got *you* out on a cold night, Mr. Tye?"

"You, Lieutenant. I came because I heard you were here."

She hesitated. She was tempted to let him have the last word. Then she realized the cameras were on her and the mikes recording.

"Any comment at this time would jeopardize the investigation," she said. Then with a quirk at the corner of her lips, she added, "You should have stayed in bed, Mr. Tye."

CHAPTER
FIVE

The segment was broadcast on the Liberty Network News that very morning at seven. It was repeated again at ten and then again at noon. Everybody who saw it got a kick out of it—for different reasons. Actually, Norah was surprised Tye decided to use it—without editing. Showed he had a sense of humor, anyway. On the second viewing, she decided that neither one of them came off badly. She even laughed herself.

The men on the squad were delighted. "Way to go, Lieut."

Roy Brennan, an old friend now working out of the general detective division of the Two-Oh, came upstairs to see her. "That's telling them, Lieutenant."

Manny Jacoby stopped by her office. "You handled that well, Norah."

She flushed. Despite an association going on to three years, Jacoby called her by her first name only on the rarest occasions. Short, balding, overweight, the precinct commander was ambitious and hard-working; dedicated and dogged. What he lacked was flair and imagination. Though he recognized his failing, he was nevertheless wary of those who were so gifted. From those instinctively talented, like Norah, he demanded strict adherence to procedure. His coming to her to express approval was unprecedented.

She was grateful, but bewildered. "Thanks, Captain, but it was no big thing."

Jacoby waggled a stubby finger. "The chief thinks otherwise."

That would be Chief of Detectives Luis Deland, of course. Norah felt her color rising. Chief Deland had the reputation of being very supportive of his people. Norah had had personal interaction with him on at least three cases. Still, she couldn't see him getting on the phone to the captain about this. Unless Jacoby had called him. She couldn't see that either. Of one thing she was sure: Manny Jacoby wouldn't be sitting in her office like this and smiling unless he had tested the climate downtown in the Big Building.

"I just wish they'd stop running the tape," she said.

"Don't worry. By tonight they'll be hitting on somebody else."

But they weren't and Norah was starting to get annoyed. She wasn't in good humor when the call came.

"Hello, Lieutenant Mulcahaney. This is Randall Tye. How do you like seeing yourself on television?"

"I'm getting tired of myself. Bored."

"That's not the reaction we're getting here at the network. People are calling in. They're delighted with you. They want to know more about you."

"I can't imagine why."

"Because you're a detective lieutenant, you're efficient, and you have style." He paused, then added, "Also, you're good-looking."

"Aha!"

"What do you mean—*aha?* What's wrong with being attractive?"

"It shouldn't enter." Norah had thought problems with women's rights were more or less behind her. She was surprised at the indignation lying dormant.

"It does, Lieutenant, and there's nothing you can do about that. You're the top female officer in the NYPD and the public likes you and is interested to know more about you."

"Wrong, Mr. Tye, on two counts. I am not the top female officer, far from it. There are females at the rank of inspector and deputy inspector. There are females at the rank of captain. I will not give you the present count on them or on lieutenants and sergeants, female, because I don't make the distinction between officer and officer female whether detective or in uniform."

"Whoa, hold it. You're right. I apologize. I was just trying to indicate that we've had a tremendous response from our viewers and it occurred to me they'd enjoy and you also might enjoy appearing as a guest on my *People in the News* program Saturday."

"You want me to appear on your show? To be interviewed?"

"Have you ever seen the show?"

"Yes, a couple of times."

"Then you know I don't take an adversary attitude toward my guests. I don't attempt to browbeat or embarrass them. I'm supportive. I invite people I think have done important work. I don't boost my ratings on somebody else's humiliation."

"Yes, I accept that, but . . . I can't do it. I have to say no. Thank you for asking me, Mr. Tye. I'm very flattered, but I can't. I have too much work."

"It'll only take an hour of your time. I'll send a car for you to your office and I'll have you delivered back to your office or anywhere else you want. What do you say, Lieutenant? Come on, be a sport."

Norah wavered for an instant, no more. "No. I can't. I don't think you understand, Mr. Tye. I couldn't answer your questions. No matter how considerate you might be, I'm not at liberty to discuss an open case, nor to give an opinion on cleared cases, for that matter."

"I'll respect that. I'm sure we can find something to talk about."

"No, I don't think so. I really don't think we can, Mr. Tye."

*   *   *

Simon Wyler didn't get home to Lola on Monday night and not on Tuesday morning either. The sun rose; the city started to dig out; Norah Mulcahaney and Fernando Arenas responded to the call at the Valente penthouse, and still he waited for Stefanie Altman's arraignment. An unwieldy, antiquated process, he thought. True, it had been even worse. Arraignment time used to run as high as twenty-eight hours in Brooklyn and fifty-nine hours in the Bronx! Since the new law had gone into effect in July 1987, there was a cap of twenty-four hours; if the prisoner was not arraigned by then, he had to be released. But even that was too much, Wyler thought, setting aside his fifth cup of lukewarm, cardboard-flavored coffee. With all the electronic gadgets, you'd think a more efficient system could be devised. He shouldn't have to be pacing the halls and waiting for the paperwork from Albany. At least, Simon consoled himself, before bringing the suspect in he had made a thorough search for the knife she claimed her attacker had wielded. It hadn't been found and he would have liked to be at the scene for another look when the plow came through. Unless that knife turned up, Wyler thought, Stefanie Altman was in big trouble.

From the time he'd put the cuffs on her, the girl hadn't said a word, only looked at him with those big, nearsighted eyes. She'd seemed totally bewildered. Under the circumstances, he couldn't blame her. That is, if her story was true.

It was four in the afternoon, a mere twelve hours from the time he'd brought her in, when the Legal Aid lawyer assigned to Altman appeared, an indication their turn was near. Along with the lawyer came her boyfriend, Timothy Kampel. Kampel brought news that Stefanie's customers and her neighbors were raising money for her bail. On the basis of her standing in the community, the judge decided she could be released on the relatively low sum, considering the charge, of one hundred thousand dollars. To Stefanie, it didn't seem much of a break.

She might have appreciated her freedom more if she'd

known the latest development. Early that afternoon, while Simon Wyler paced and Stefanie sat dazed in a holding cell, Lieutenant Mulcahaney ordered a ballistics team to return to the scene. One bullet, the one that had passed through Frank Beech's heart, had been recovered by the ME. The ballistics detectives found a second lodged in the concrete of the third step down from the landing. The implication was clear, but Wyler wanted to take another look himself. While Kampel was dealing with the bail bondsman, he returned to Seventy-sixth Street.

The Sanitation Department plow had already been through. It had cut a narrow swath down the middle of the road for traffic and in so doing had pushed the snow into huge banks along both sides. Children, young and old, were out playing and squealing with delight. They used the banks as fortresses for a snowball fight; the little ones climbed to the top and slid down on what looked like giant Frisbees. Wyler just sighed. Whatever was underneath the snow would stay there a long time. He reminded himself that the knife was not what he had come here about. He walked up the block to Altman's house and climbed to the top of the landing.

Everything had been shoveled clean. The bullet had been pried out of the concrete by Ballistics, naturally, but the place where it had lodged was easy to discern. Wyler recreated the shooting in his mind. The girl and Beech up here; the other two guys on the pavement below. She had shot directly at Beech, she admitted that. But for the bullet to have passed through his body and lodged in the steps below, he had to have been down already. No way to get around that. Beech had to have sustained one shot, the fatal shot through the heart, had to have been down on his knees in front of her when she fired the second time. A scenario not calculated to arouse sympathy.

And how about the other shots? She claimed she'd fired without intent to injure, that she'd only meant to scare the other two men off. She could have fired over their heads, to the right or left, high or low. She didn't remember, and Wyler was faced with those embankments of

snow. He shivered. The wind was picking up and twilight
fading into night. Mothers called their children inside, and
the street quieted. Might as well forget about locating the
other bullets, he thought.

"What you doing, mister?"

A chubby boy wrapped in layers of sweaters, with a
knitted cap pulled low to his eyes and a muffler wound
high to his nose, stood at the bottom of the steps.

"I'm a detective. I'm investigating."

"The shooting yesterday?"

He was about eleven or twelve, hard to tell with him
bundled up like that, Wyler thought. His brash curiosity
suggested he might be in his teens; on the other hand,
there was a hint of the timidity of a younger child. He was
certainly lonely or he would have been playing with one
of the groups and have gone inside. Lonely children saw
a lot.

"You know about the shooting?"

"I heard the shots. I saw guys running. One of them
fell down right in front of my house."

"Where's your house?"

The boy extended his right arm. "Around the corner."

Last night's canvass had not gone beyond this one
block. Wyler's spirits rose. "How many guys did you see?"

"Two."

"And what made you think they had anything to do
with the shooting?"

"One guy yelled: 'I'm shot, I'm shot.' "

"Are you sure he said that?"

The boy nodded.

"Then what happened?"

"The other man helped him up and they made it to the
subway."

"What time was all this? Do you remember?"

"Sure. It was before supper."

"I see. And how many shots did you hear?"

The boy hesitated. "I don't know. A lot."

Wyler decided that to press him might confuse him.
"What's your name, son?"

"Bobby Lash."

"Okay, Bobby, where were you when you observed all this?"

"In my room, looking out the window."

"You say the men made it to the subway. Did you actually see them go down the stairs?"

"They started down."

"Did the man who had fallen seem badly hurt?"

Bobby Lash shrugged; the young have little sympathy for others' pain, Wyler thought. "He limped. He was leaning on his buddy."

"Which leg was he favoring?"

The child shook his head.

"Could you describe the men? The one who limped— how was he dressed?" Wyler knew that it had been dark and the snow had made visibility more difficult; he was testing the boy.

"Am I going to have to give evidence in court?" Bobby Lash was both excited and anxious.

Not only because of the language he'd used, but because of the very fact that the possibility had occurred to him, Wyler decided he had to be in his teens. "Would you be able to?"

"Suppose he comes after me?"

They learn fear early, Wyler thought. "Don't worry, he's not going to know a thing about you." He pulled a card out of his wallet. "There's my name and phone number. If you remember anything else about last night, you get in touch. Okay?"

A look of greed displaced the fear. "Is there a reward?"

Simon Wyler knew Bobby Lash couldn't identify the two men he had observed from his window. He was interested in the boy's story because it supported Altman's contention that there were three men involved, not one. The man Bobby Lash saw fall and the man who helped him up could have been two innocent citizens making their way through the storm to the subway. The boy's statement that he'd heard the cry *"I'm shot, I'm shot"* could be overactive imagination. Was there some way of proving the truth of it? If the man had in fact been shot, the blood was long since washed out in the snow. But he would have required treatment, wouldn't he?

As soon as he returned to the squad room, Wyler got to work on the telephone. In less than an hour he had the information he wanted. Shortly after seven the night before, the ER at Presbyterian Medical Center in Washington Heights reported treating a male Caucasian, twenty-four years old, for a gunshot wound in the left thigh. Wyler was elated. Luck combined with logic and dogged routine had brought him this far and then he got lucky once more. The injury had been only a flesh wound and like most such wounds had bled profusely. Ordinarily, such a patient would have been expected to give a false ID, pay out of his pocket, and get away before the police arrived. Only this time, the victim had no money on him and the sight of his own blood flowing panicked him into telling the truth so that his mother could come and get him.

His name was Carl Pesrow and he lived on Staten Island.

Wyler felt a tingling in his blood. He wanted to get on a ferry and go right out there. But it was nearly 9:00 P.M. He'd been on duty twenty-nine hours. He'd already logged too much overtime, but the lieut didn't favor the pass-along system. Neither did he. He was the one who'd found Pesrow and he wanted to be the one to bring him in. If Pesrow had had any intention of skipping he would be long gone anyway, Wyler reasoned, so tomorrow would be time enough. He would go home for that quiet dinner with Lola and go to bed.

As it turned out, he was saved the ferry ride. The next morning, Carl Pesrow came to him. With his lawyer. And that was when Simon Wyler's luck ran out.

Pesrow was a skinny youth with a bad complexion and long, greasy brown hair pulled back in a ponytail and secured with a rubber band. He had a pinched, pointy nose like Pinocchio's before he started to lie, except that from the shifty look of him Carl Pesrow had been lying from the time he started to talk. Certainly, he wasn't the type to enter a police station willingly unless he had something to gain. The first clue was that he came with his leg in a cast and using crutches. The second was that his lawyer, Milo Vanderberg, was known to get the bulk of his business by prowling the courthouse halls and approaching bewildered first-time offenders. Who had solicited whom? Wyler wondered.

"We're here to file a complaint," Milo Vanderberg announced aggressively.

Wyler waved them to chairs. As he rolled the standard form into the typewriter, he noted the exaggerated care Vanderberg took of his client. Having elicited name and address and noted the time of filing, he addressed Pesrow.

"All right, Mr. Pesrow, what's the problem?"

"I've been shot. The crazy woman shot me. All we wanted was to know where's the nearest subway—and she starts spraying the street with bullets."

"Slow down, Mr. Pesrow. Slow down. When were you shot?"

"Monday night. The night of the blizzard."

Wyler, a good typist, quickly tapped it out. "Time?"

"Around six. Yeah, six."

"P.M.?" At Pesrow's nod he added that. "Where?"

"Where? In the leg, man, in the leg. You've got eyes! Could have been a lot more serious. They told me at the hospital that a couple of inches over and it would have punctured one of the main arteries. I could have bled to death. That's what they said." Then as lawyer Vanderberg leaned over and whispered, he became less truculent. "Oh, you mean where. Yeah, I get ya. Seventy-sixth, like half a block up from Columbus."

It had been smart coaching not to let him glibly state which brownstone, Wyler thought. "And what were you doing on Seventy-sixth just off Columbus on Monday night in the middle of a snowstorm, Mr. Pesrow?" he asked.

"Trying to find a subway and get back down to the ferry and get home. We didn't know the neighborhood. We were lost. It was coming down so hard you couldn't see more than a couple of yards ahead. We were just putting one foot in front of the other when we spotted this woman climbing up the steps of one of the houses. We figured she lived there so she must know where the subway was. We called out to her and ran to catch up before she went inside."

Pausing, Carl Pesrow cast a look at his attorney, who responded with a barely perceptible nod of encouragement. "She started to yell: 'Leave me alone! Don't touch me!' Like that. Hell, we weren't anywhere close to her. Frank goes up to try to calm her and explain all we want is directions and suddenly she's got a piece in her hand. Without another word, she fires and Frank goes down. He kind of balances on his knees for a couple of seconds, then he falls sideways and rolls over and over, down the steps to the sidewalk and into the gutter. That's not enough for her; she fires at us!" Pesrow paused to let both the detective and his lawyer appreciate his indignation. "I mean, we're nowhere near her.

"So what can we do? We have to leave Frank behind and run for our lives. I'm damn lucky she got me where she did. They told me at the hospital a couple of inches over . . ."

"Yes, yes, I understand." Wyler stanched the flow of self-pity. "May I ask why you didn't come forward sooner to lodge this complaint?"

"Man, I was sick. I was weak. I lost a lot of blood. Haven't you been listening?"

Wyler managed to contain himself. "This woman who shot you, could you identify her?"

"Sure. That's why I'm here. Her picture was in the paper. It's the same one who killed Frank."

"Then you're also here as a witness."

Pesrow looked to his lawyer openly. This was a question for which apparently he had not rehearsed an answer.

"Mr. Pesrow is prepared to do his duty as a citizen,"

Vanderberg replied silkily. "But he is also seeking justice on his own account."

Were they going to sue? Wyler wondered. Were they going to try to sue Stefanie Altman? Was that what this was all about? How could they? On what grounds? Besides, Altman had no money. A man as conniving as Milo Vanderberg had surely informed himself about her financial situation before getting involved. His client, Carl Pesrow, certainly had no money for legal fees, so what was in it for Vanderberg? Publicity! Wyler thought, answering his own question, more publicity than a small-time ambulance chaser could ever dream of.

They come out of the cracks, Wyler thought as he finished the complaint form and pulled it out of the typewriter. Separating the copies, he handed one to Pesrow. "Look it over and see if you want to add or change anything. I'll be right back."

He went over to the lieutenant's office and knocked on her door. Told to enter, he went in and handed Norah the recently filled-out complaint along with the hospital report on Pesrow's injury. "I thought you'd want to talk to him yourself. He's got his lawyer with him."

"Has he?"

The introductions were brief. Pesrow seemed shaken to be facing an officer of Norah's rank. Vanderberg, of course, had set his sights even higher. So Norah addressed him first.

"You do know, Mr. Vanderberg, that the woman against whom your client is lodging his complaint already faces a possible murder charge?"

"She's out!" Pesrow exclaimed. "How come you turned her loose?"

"She's been released on bail pending a hearing by the grand jury."

"Does that mean I have to wait in line for my turn?"

Deliberately Norah looked over the paper in her hand. "According to your statement, you recognized the woman who shot you from a picture in the paper. What paper?"

"The *Post*. Yesterday's late edition."

He had volunteered something he shouldn't have, Norah thought. She remembered the piece and she remembered that the photograph had been a graduation portrait of Stefanie Altman. "Can you describe the woman?"

"Sure." A big grin broke out on the youth's pimply face; he was ready for this. "She was thin. She had brown hair, long brown hair. She had big, bulgy eyes. Also she had a mole up on her right cheek . . ."

"Just a minute, Mr. Pesrow," Norah interrupted. "You're describing the woman in the photograph. I want to know what the woman looked like on the night you actually saw her, on the night you claim she shot you."

"Oh." A startled look to his lawyer brought no help. "Well, she was . . ." He grimaced. "She was all bundled up for one thing . . . She had on this down coat, a kind of purple color. And a hat, a knitted hat. It was pulled way down to her eyebrows. She had glasses."

"You're describing what she was wearing, Mr. Pesrow. Now tell us what she looked like."

"Considering the circumstances—the poor visibility, the stress of the situation—Mr. Pesrow has done remarkably well," Vanderberg came to his client's aid.

Pesrow nodded vigorously. "All I know is she killed Frank and damn near killed me." He put a hand on the cast and flinched as though the wound were fresh. "Anyway, she's admitted it, hasn't she?"

It was a statement and Norah ignored it. "You're testifying that you and Frank Beech and another man approached Ms. Altman for the purpose of asking directions. That was your sole intent."

"That's right."

"You never threatened her?" Wyler asked suddenly.

Pesrow spun around. "Never."

"What were you doing in Manhattan? What were you doing on Seventy-sixth Street?" Norah asked.

Pesrow swiveled back to her. "Me and Frank came over to look for work."

It was Wyler's turn. "How long did you know each other?"

"Since we were kids. We grew up together," Pesrow explained, and automatically turned to Norah for the next question.

"Go on," Wyler said.

"We hit a couple of the employment agencies downtown, but we had no luck. Then we heard there was temporary work at a big carpet warehouse on Seventy-eighth and Broadway. By the time we got there, the jobs were filled. So we had us a couple of beers and started for home. Only by then it was snowing so hard we got all turned around. We saw this woman up ahead and we hailed her. But she wouldn't stop. She wouldn't wait for us."

It could have happened like that. It was a reasonable account, Norah thought. The men at least mildly drunk, the girl growing increasingly alarmed as they persisted. "Then what happened?"

"She ran up the stairs of one of the houses and Frank ran up after her. The next thing I knew she had a gun in her hand. Frank was down. She started shooting in all directions."

"How about the ski mask?" Norah asked. "When did he put that on?"

Again Pesrow looked to his attorney and again Vanderberg was at a loss.

"A ski mask was found beside Beech's body," she told them.

"So?" Vanderberg shrugged.

"So it wasn't snowing when you and Frank left Staten Island on Monday morning," she reminded Pesrow. "Frank wasn't wearing boots. Were you?"

The complainant shook his head, confused.

"You weren't dressed for the snow, were you? Neither one of you?"

"No," he admitted, still uncertain of where all this was going.

"So how did Frank Beech just happen to have a ski mask? You had one too, didn't you?"

"Don't answer," Vanderberg snapped. "You know better than to ask him that, Lieutenant."

Norah took up another line. "There were three of you. Who's the third man? What's his name?"

"Dan."

"Dan what?"

"I don't know. Never saw him before. An old guy. In his fifties. We were sitting around at the agency down near Battery Park, me and Frank, and we got to talking to the other guys—comparing notes, you know. This Dan, he was the one knew about the jobs uptown at the carpet warehouse."

"You don't know where this Dan lives?"

"No."

"He was a stranger, yet he helped you to the subway when you were shot."

"That's right. He went with me and got me to Presbyterian."

Wyler pounced. "So he knew where the subway was."

"We found it by accident."

"Why go all the way up to Presbyterian?" Wyler persisted.

"It was his choice. Maybe because the first train that pulled in was headed up there."

"Okay, so he got you there and then . . ."

"He left."

"Just like that?"

Pesrow shrugged.

"What it amounts to, Mr. Pesrow, is that you've got nobody to back up your story," Wyler summed up. "It's your word against Ms. Altman's."

"She's the one who had the gun. She's the one who did the shooting," Vanderberg stated hotly, winding up for a harangue.

"If Mr. Pesrow will give us the name of the employment agency he and Frank Beech applied to on Monday morning, we'll check out the story," Norah sought to calm him.

"Sure, I can do that. I cut the ad out of the Sunday papers and I got it right here." He fumbled in his pocket and produced a much-battered wallet and from that drew a neatly trimmed newspaper box advertisement by the Acme Agency for part-time and full-time office and industrial personnel. He passed it over to Norah. He seemed quite pleased with himself.

"Thank you," she said. "Thank you for coming in."

"That's it?"

"For now. Don't forget to sign the complaint."

Wyler showed them out.

He came back quickly. He was excited and now he could let it show.

"How about the mole on Altman's right cheek, Lieutenant? He got that from the picture in the paper. She doesn't have it anymore. She had it removed a long time ago."

Norah nodded. "His lawyer outsmarted himself."

"Pesrow can identify Altman, that's for sure," Wyler concluded with satisfaction. Then his face clouded. "Problem is—is that good or bad for our side?"

"We don't have a side, Simon," she reminded him quietly.

"You know what I mean, Lieutenant."

"Sure." Norah sighed. "Sure I do." She handed him the newspaper clipping. "You'd better get over to Acme and see if the story checks out."

CHAPTER
SIX

Captain Jacoby did not call on Norah in her office the next morning: he summoned her to his.

"I hear Randall Tye invited you to go on his *People in the News* show and you turned him down."

Blunt and to the point: Back to normal, Norah thought. What surprised her was not Jacoby's attitude, but that Tye had gone over her head. Somehow, she hadn't expected it from him. It wouldn't do him any good, though. She squared her shoulders and raised her chin. "That's right, Captain."

"The chief thinks you should change your mind. He thinks it would be good PR for the department for you to appear. We've been getting bad press lately. We could use some favorable exposure."

The chief! Norah hadn't credited Tye with being able to reach up that far. Undoubtedly, the network had done it for him, but either way, he'd taken the choice out of her hands. She wasn't going to forget it. She wasn't giving in, either. "Captain, I honestly don't have the time. We're carrying two big cases here."

"Two?"

"Yes, sir. The Altman and Valente homicides. Stefanie Altman is the woman who was accosted on the front steps of her house and shot the would-be mugger."

"The alleged mugger," Jacoby corrected, and Norah flushed. "I know the case; you don't need to review it for me. You don't need to refresh me on the Valente case either," he added. "Altman's going before the grand jury this coming Monday. What's the problem?"

"We haven't got all the evidence."

"The knife she claims he threatened her with?" Jacoby asked. "The snow's all melted or been removed by now. Whatever was or wasn't under it is gone."

"One of the other men could have taken it," Norah pointed out. "Anyhow, there is a third man involved. We should hear his testimony. We haven't done any real background on . . . Beech." She had started to say—the victim.

Jacoby shrugged. "I don't hear the DA complaining. All right, all right, you're not through with the investigation. Agreed. But how long can this appearance on the Randall Tye show take? A couple of hours?"

It would be less trouble not to argue, Norah decided. "If it's an order from Chief Deland . . ."

"Not an order, Lieutenant Mulcahaney, a suggestion."

Same thing—and they both knew it. "Yes, Captain."

So Norah informed Tye's office that she would be available after all and the appearance was scheduled for that Saturday. As soon as she hung up, Norah started getting nervous. Why did she have to do this? Why couldn't somebody else go on the show? Chief Deland himself? Jim Felix? Anybody? Norah had been in the spotlight before; she'd dealt with the press, but never before had she been the subject of an interview by a top television reporter, a celebrity in his own right, on national television. For the rest of the day, no matter what she was doing, she couldn't put it out of her mind.

Damn, Norah thought, I'll never get through it. Maybe I could say I was sick? No, then I couldn't come to work. Suppose I had laryngitis? That would only result in postponement. She would have to go through with it, she decided, so she might as well get it over now. She believed that she was resigned to the ordeal but at the next ring of the phone she had a surge of hope: Maybe Tye had found somebody more important and couldn't fit her in. By then even a postponement would have been a reprieve.

It was Phil Worgan.

"I've got some interesting news for you."

Norah sat up, alert, Randall Tye and the show forgotten.

"There's no question that Gilda Valente's death was caused by drowning. Her lungs were filled with chlorinated water from the pool. Taking into account the temperature and the stomach contents from her last known meal, a light lunch at noon, death appears to have occurred between ten and twelve that night." The briskness of his manner indicated those were the preliminaries. "Also"—he paused—"she was pregnant." He waited. "Are you with me, Norah?"

"Yes, yes. I didn't expect this. The Valentes' marriage was touted as ideal. An example to all. The only flaw in their happiness was that they didn't have a child."

"One was on the way."

Norah sighed. "Is it possible she didn't know?"

"After three months?"

"Her husband didn't mention it. The man was stricken by grief. He went through a terrible ordeal and nearly died himself in the effort to get back here and find out for himself what happened. He came to avenge his wife's death. If he had known she was carrying his child, a child he'd given up hope of ever having, I think he would have done more than mention it." She paused. "Unless, of course, she didn't tell him."

"I can't say about that," Worgan replied. "But Valente just called and asked for a copy of the autopsy report. I got the feeling that the content has been leaked and he wants to confirm it. Naturally, I told him he'd have to speak to you. You'll be hearing from him. Soon."

"Thanks, Phil."

And not more than ten minutes later the call did come.

"Lieutenant Mulcahaney?" He didn't bother to identify himself; maybe because he thought his voice was distinctive enough, or he knew she had been warned to expect the call. "I want a copy of the autopsy report."

"I was on the point of contacting you, Mr. Valente. I can come over right away, if that's convenient."

There was a barely perceptible hesitation before he said *yes* and hung up.

The climate of cooperation was becoming strained.

As on her previous visits, Salvatore Nunzio was waiting to admit Norah. He greeted her with the customary courtesy.

"Mr. Valente is in the study."

As they passed the dining room, Norah was aware of a shadow at the partially opened door, a shadow that was gone before Norah could identify it. The soft closing of the door was the only confirmation that someone had actually been there.

Nunzio said nothing; perhaps he hadn't noticed. At the study, he knocked, passed Norah in, and then withdrew.

Dario Valente was dressed casually but elegantly in gray slacks of fine British wool and a sweater vest over a gray shirt of Italian silk. He was pale. The swelling and bruises on one side of his face had faded into a large yellow smudge; the cuts and scratches on the other side were dried up and had almost disappeared. He still looked drawn, but Norah was surprised at the extent of his recovery in a mere thirty-six hours. He had a strong constitution, she thought; he was as strong in body as in will. A man of whom to be wary. He made no pretense that he was doing anything other than waiting for her, nor did he try to minimize the extent of his anxiety. Brusquely, he waved her to a chair.

"I might as well tell you I've heard rumors of what's in the autopsy report." He looked at Norah's shoulder-strap handbag.

He didn't volunteer how the information had reached him and she didn't ask. "I don't have the report, Mr. Valente. I haven't seen it, but I have been officially informed of its contents." She took a breath. "Your wife died between ten and twelve on the night of November thirtieth. She was three months pregnant."

His face sagged some more. It was his only evident reaction. "There's no possibility of error?"

"None."

Then he turned away. A twitch of his broad shoulders was the only indication of his emotion. However, when, after a long awkward wait, he did turn to her once more, Norah saw its ravages: reddened eyes, the runnels of tears; the dazed look sudden disaster leaves.

"I couldn't understand why anybody would want to kill Gilda. I dismissed the possibility that anybody would want to hurt me through her. But if she was pregnant, then by killing her they killed my seed. My God, Lieutenant, do you know what that means to me?"

"Yes, I do." Her own sorrow and Joe's at not being able to have a child would never be forgotten.

"I'm going to get the man who did this," Valente vowed. "I'm going to rip his guts out with my bare hands."

"You didn't know your wife was pregnant?"

"No."

"Forgive me, Mr. Valente, it seems strange she didn't tell you. I would have thought . . ."

"That I might have guessed? I'd stopped guessing, Lieutenant. We had been disappointed twice before, you see. Twice before we'd had our hopes raised. This time she must have been waiting to make absolutely sure so as not to disappoint me again."

"Yes, I see. But she must have told someone, that is if the motive for killing her was to kill the child she was carrying." The thought brought a cold chill.

Valente scowled. "Her doctor would have known, of course. His nurse. The lab that processed the test."

"The test would carry a number rather than a name."

"It should be investigated."

"It will be," Norah assured him. "How about a friend? Did Mrs. Valente have a woman friend she might have been likely to confide in?"

"No. Gilda knew a lot of people; she served on many charitable committees; she was on the board of the Metropolitan Museum and the Metropolitan Opera, but friends of the kind you suggest . . . Wait. How stupid! There's Armanda, of course. She was a second mother to Gilda." He pressed a button on the small telephone console.

Seconds later, so quickly it seemed she must have been waiting for the summons, there was a light tap at the door and Mrs. Sequi entered. She wore the same plain black dress she had worn before, but it seemed more than ever the vestment of mourning. She cast a quick, sideways glance at Norah, then, lowering her eyes, took two small steps into the room and stationed herself before Valente like a servant rather than a member of the family.

Valente let her stand there.

"Did Gilda tell you she was pregnant?"

She flinched as though she'd been slapped and she gasped for breath. Her raddled cheeks quivered. *"Incinta? No, non me l'ha mai detto. Non lo sapevo. Incinta? Sei sicuro?"*

Valente's face darkened. *"I dottori sono sicuri,"* he retorted. Then suddenly he seemed to remember who she was and got up and went around the desk. Gently, he put his arm around her. "We must speak in English, *cara.*"

The woman swallowed and nodded.

"Did Mrs. Valente tell you she was pregnant?" Norah asked.

"No. I didn't know. I had no idea. *O, Dio mio.*" She dropped her head into her hands and began to weep.

"Stai tranquilla. Sarà vendicata." Without asking Norah if she needed more from Mrs. Sequi, Valente led her to the door and handed her over to someone outside.

Norah waited till the door was shut again. "I would like to go over the events of Monday night with you once more, Mr. Valente."

"I remind you that I wasn't here, Lieutenant."

"The events as they relate directly to you. Your movements, in other words."

He raised his hands in frustration and then dropped

them. "I have gone over them half a dozen times—with you, with the assistant district attorney, the FBI, and so on and on, but I will go over them a thousand more times if it will help."

"You had been at your country place most of the preceding week, alone?"

"For five days, yes. Gilda didn't like to rough it. Long walks in the woods didn't appeal to her. Also, she had all kinds of social commitments—committee meetings, lunches, that kind of thing—scheduled."

"I see. But you had planned to return to the city on Monday. Any particular reason?"

"No." He allowed himself a wry smile. "I have to admit that after a few days up there I get bored myself. And lonely." He sighed.

"Then why did you change your mind?"

"The predicted storm. Over our way the first flurries started at noon. It intensified so quickly that by two in the afternoon the local airport was closed. I didn't think I could make it driving and I certainly didn't want to risk getting stranded. So I called Gilda and told her I wouldn't be home till the next day."

"So you called a little after two?" Valente nodded. "What had your original plans been?"

He took so long to answer that she was about ready to repeat the question.

"Nothing special. A quiet evening at home."

"Is it possible the perpetrator expected to find you home on Monday night?"

"He came looking for me? You mean I was the intended victim?" Dario Valente appeared stunned. "I never thought of that. My God, it could be. He came for me and he found Gilda, alone, swimming. She was frightened. She screamed. She tried to get out of the pool and to the intercom to call the guards downstairs. He grabbed her and pushed her back into the water. He held her under . . ."

It could have happened like that, Norah thought. "There's no guard at the service entrance after six, but he would still have needed a key."

Valente sighed. "My security is simple but effective, Lieutenant, and I trust my people. However, if somebody is determined enough, the best security can be breached."

That was certainly true, she thought. "Have you any idea who it might have been?"

"I have many enemies, as I've told you before."

"Yes." Norah got up. "And I remind you that we have a deal and that any information you get you've agreed to turn over to me."

Valente drew himself up. "I gave you my word."

Norah left by the back so she could check the route. In doing so, she realized that in addition to the keys for the service entrance and service elevator, a key to the back door of the penthouse would also be required. If the perpetrator could get two, then he could also get the third, she reasoned. What concerned Norah was the quickness with which Valente had accepted her suggestion that the killer had come looking for him, not his wife. Instantly he had presented a credible sequence of events. There was, however, another slant that she hadn't presented. In fact, this alternative interpretation was so obvious Norah was surprised it hadn't occurred to the *capo*. Or maybe it had.

CHAPTER
SEVEN

Gilda Valente was beautiful and rich, but of common stock and married to a prince of organized crime. Money, however, is a great equalizer, and by dint of substantial contributions, Gilda Valente had bought her way to a place on one prestigious committee, then another, and another. In this way her name began to be linked with those born to privilege.

These were the people Norah Mulcahaney now sought to interrogate. She started with the Committee for Shelter for Homeless Families, one of the many on which Mrs. Valente had served. The chairman would not make himself available, so she had to settle for Montgomery Ashford, assistant to the chairman. Paid assistant. Nevertheless, as soon as Norah walked into the small, well-ordered office maintained by the committee she realized she was in luck and that it was Ashford who actually ran things and who would be not only better disposed but better able than the titular head to help her. Also, he was a stylish young man whose supercilious manner masked an intense curiosity about and envy of the people for whom he worked. In other words, ideal for Norah's purpose.

"I'm genuinely distressed about Mrs. Valente's demise," Montgomery Ashford intoned. "She was not only a beautiful woman but a truly beautiful human being. Her nomination to the committee met with considerable resistance, but she made a large contribution and it was not possible to turn her down. Nobody really expected her to appear at meetings, not after the first time. Most ladies like to be listed as patrons on the letterheads, the official program, and so forth. They appear on the night of the benefit in sables and diamonds, but they never do anything as ordinary as attend meetings. So Mrs. Valente surprised everyone. She not only came regularly, she accepted whatever job she was assigned and did it well. She never once complained it wasn't big enough or important enough."

"So she made friends."

Ashford pursed his lips. "In the sense you mean, Lieutenant, I don't think so."

Norah couldn't hint, suggest, or in any way even appear to lead the witness. Ashford was much too prudent to volunteer the information, so she had to ask straight out.

"Did she have any enemies?"

"I don't know of anybody who wanted to kill her."

"What about her marriage? Was it a happy one?"

"I never heard it wasn't. Of my own personal knowledge and observation, I saw them together perhaps three or four times at formal dinners and balls. They were never other than radiant."

More than prudent, Norah thought, cautious.

She moved on to the Committee for Assistance to Teen-age Mothers.

"We'll miss her," Mrs. Hildegarde Marsh told Norah. Mrs. Marsh received Norah in a comfortable, well-appointed office, part of the suite belonging to Crown Texas Oil in the World Trade Center. Mrs. Marsh was on the board of Crown and the actual chairperson of the committee. Tiny, silver-haired, she was a dynamo eighty-one years young. There was no doubt who ran that operation.

"We'll miss her," Mrs. Marsh repeated, and there was genuine affection in her tone and her look. "Gilda Valente was a lovely young woman. Caring. A hard worker. Never missed a meeting." She caught herself up. "Well, so rarely it didn't matter."

Apparently regular attendance was a highly regarded indication of sincerity, Norah thought. "I suppose you keep minutes that show the attendance. Could you tell me how many meetings Mrs. Valente may have missed in . . . the last six months?"

Organized and knowledgeable as Mrs. Marsh was, she had to call her secretary for that. Scanning the record, she quickly ascertained that Gilda Valente had missed only four sessions since June, making it about one Thursday out of six.

"Did she mention why she wasn't able to attend?" Norah asked.

The little aristocrat pursed her lips. "She wasn't required to do so."

Norah accepted the rebuff. She had been probing at random and some instinct told her to persist. "What time of day are the meetings usually held and how long do they last?"

"They are luncheon meetings. We eat upstairs in the private dining room and we have the use of the board room afterward. We break up anywhere from three to five in the afternoon."

"May I have a list of the members?"

"Certainly. We call them Benefactors."

"Was there friction between Mrs. Valente and any of the others?"

"If you're asking whether I know of anyone who might have wanted to kill her, the answer is no. I repeat, she was a lovely young woman in every sense."

"And her marriage was happy?"

"Did you know that Gilda was raised to be Dario Valente's bride?" Hildegarde Marsh asked. "She was fifteen years old when Dario first laid eyes on her. He was on a visit to the old country and she had just been orphaned. Her parents and grandparents were killed in a car crash. She had no one. She was about to be turned over to the state and placed in an orphanage when Valente intervened. He arranged for Armanda Sequi to officially adopt the girl and paid her to care for Gilda. Over the years, he made several trips back to Agrigento, ostensibly on business, yet he never failed to look in and observe her progress. At nineteen, Gilda was brought over and they were married."

"So Mrs. Sequi is not her real aunt."

"No, she is Mr. Valente's aunt."

"Ah. May I ask how you came by this information?" Norah asked.

"From Gilda," Mrs. Marsh told her. "People frequently commented on the difference in age between her and Dario Valente. Unkindly, I'm sorry to say. One of our own committee members was guilty of unseemly gossip and she overheard him. She didn't waste any time putting him straight. She admitted the marriage was arranged, but she said such a marriage had more chance of success than one based on mere physical attraction, on a chance falling in love. She told him she cared deeply about her husband and did nothing without first weighing how it would affect him. She ended by wishing the committee member as much success in his marriage as she had in hers."

The little woman's eyes gleamed mischievously. "The man is a perennial bachelor."

Norah moved on. She continued her investigation into Gilda Valente's past, visiting, among others, the Committee for In-Home Care for the Aged and the Committee for the Gala Fund Raiser for remodeling the Vivian Beaumont Theatre at Lincoln Center (yet again). The interviews were mere repetitions. Gilda Valente had established a reputation as a hard worker. Her attendance record was much admired. No one questioned the infrequent absences. But charting them, Norah perceived a pattern. They added up to one per week regularly, though each was on a different day. What did she do on those days when she skipped a meeting? Norah wondered. Where did she go? Whom did she meet?

It could be nothing more than a date at the hairdresser, an extra session at the aerobics class that she attended sporadically, or a dress rehearsal at the Met where she was listed as a participant in the Golden Horseshoe Program, the only one of her activities not regularly scheduled. It could also simply have been a day to herself to think, to walk, to get away. Norah compared the lists she'd requested at each headquarters and found many names duplicated, male and female. Still, it would take days to interview each person. She called in Ferdi Arenas and handed him the sheet. "I want a general portrait of each one of these people: age, background, marital status. I'm interested in gossip and rumors."

"You think Gilda had a lover?"

"Everybody seems to have accepted the marriage as ideal. Perfect." She shrugged. "Maybe it was. One thing's for sure—if she was having an affair, she knew how to cover her tracks."

Ferdi left. Norah propped her elbows on the desk, cupped her chin in her hands, and let her mind go blank. Time passed, but nothing came to fill it. She was trying to summon up instinct, to use instinct as a shortcut. But instinct didn't come on command; it came as a result of hard work, of the dogged gathering of facts. She should be out learning more about Valente and his young wife. Until she knew everything instinct was only guesswork.

The phone rang. She answered it and sat bolt upright.

"Lieutenant Mulcahaney? I'm the assistant stage manager for the *People in the News* . . ."

Norah didn't listen to the rest of it. The show was due to be taped live on Saturday. She looked at the calendar. That was tomorrow. Already? She'd managed somehow to put it out of her mind, but now Norah's stomach tightened into a hard knot.

"Lieutenant? I'm sorry to disturb you at work, but I tried your home and you weren't there." The assistant sounded young and harassed.

"No problem. What can I do for you?"

The assistant was flustered by the unexpected cooperation. "Actually, I just wanted to remind you that dress rehearsal is tomorrow at seven. Do you require transportation? If so, where would you like us to pick you up?"

"No, that's all right. I can get there on my own, but I don't think I can make it at seven."

There was a sharp intake of breath at the other end of the line. "It's scheduled for seven, Lieutenant Mulcahaney. It's set."

"But the show isn't till nine, is it?"

"That's when we go on the air, ma'am. But you have to rehearse." The assistant stage manager's voice rose in pitch.

"I thought all it was going to be was Mr. Tye asking me some questions."

"Don't you want to know what the questions will be?" The man almost pleaded.

"Yes. Yes, actually that would be good. You can send me a list."

Norah hung up.

In fact she was busy at seven on Saturday night. She had managed to get Dr. Rafaele Ruggiero, Gilda Valente's gynecologist, to agree to see her, and the time was of his choosing—certainly, she had no intention of asking him to change it. She arrived early, but he kept her waiting past the appointed hour. When he finally did receive her, the doctor offered no explanation for the lateness and Norah knew better than to ask.

"Mr. Valente has requested I cooperate with you, Lieutenant."

"Thank you. I appreciate it."

"You understand that there's a doctor-patient relationship that I cannot overstep regardless of how much I want to help."

"I don't intend—"

"Also, I'm pressed for time."

"Then suppose we get to it, Doctor," Norah replied, matching his briskness. "When was the last time Mrs. Valente consulted you?"

"The start of the summer." The physician was tall, thin,

supercilious, and efficient. He had the patient file folder at hand and he opened it to the precise place of his own notation. "Yes, here it is. June fourth. We had thought she might be pregnant, but the test came back negative. For the second time. She was very disappointed."

"And she didn't consult you again?"

"No. Therefore I couldn't have known she was pregnant when she died. That is what you wanted to know, isn't it?"

It was certainly what Dario Valente had wanted her to find out.

As she walked out of the gynecologist's private entrance directly to the sidewalk, Norah was approached by a uniformed chauffeur. He touched his cap.

"I'm from the Liberty Network News, Lieutenant. I'm to take you to the studio."

Norah frowned. How had they found out where she was? None of her people would have disclosed the information; she was sure of that. Probably, the PR man for the show had contacted his opposite number at the police PR, who, in turn, must have gone up pretty high to get clearance to reveal Dr. Ruggiero's connection to the case. If she'd had any doubts left of the importance the brass was attaching to this appearance on the Randall Tye show, they were dispelled.

"Thank you, but I have my own car." She indicated the recently purchased silver-gray Volvo parked across the street.

"I'll have it driven home for you, Lieutenant. It will be there after the show." The chauffeur held his hand out for the keys.

Norah could only grin. She opened her purse, found the car keys, and dropped them into his open palm. Then as he held the door for her, she stepped into the limousine.

CHAPTER
EIGHT

Until that morning, Norah had been too concentrated on the Altman and Valente investigations to even think about the show. During the intervening hours, she had managed to set most of her qualms aside. But they could no longer be ignored. In the ten-minute drive to the studio all of her early fears returned and got worse. Delivered to the stage entrance, she was rushed to makeup. Her stomach started to churn. Next, she was passed to the hairdresser. The look on the woman's face didn't help.

Swiftly, the stylist whipped off the ribbon that held Norah's hair, gave her a vigorous brushing that made her scalp tingle, then put the ribbon back on as it had been.

"Sorry. There's really nothing else we can do in the time."

Norah's palms were sweating.

A young woman, one of the numerous assistants scurrying around hugging clipboards, was waiting impatiently to collect Norah. She wore T-shirt, jeans, sneakers—no makeup; she was aggressively unglamorous. "I won't be able to walk you through your positions, Lieutenant. The show's already on the air. I'll just take you where you can get a look at the set."

In the form of an apology, it was actually a reprimand, or as close as any of them were permitted to administer to a guest, Norah thought as she allowed herself to be led through a forest of light stands, a maze of cables, stacks of flats to a vantage point from where she could look out on the brightly lit stage and see Randall Tye casually lounging, ugly-handsome face intent, conducting the interview with the first of his guests.

Norah's heart pounded.

The next thing she knew she was being handed over to yet another assistant. This one, a man of indeterminate age, suave and harried at the same time, was in charge of the Green Room.

"Is that what she's going to wear?" he appealed to the escort, who shrugged and got away.

Dressing that morning, Norah had thought about the show; it had not been completely out of her mind. She'd assumed she'd have time to get back home and change. She had simply put on one of her standard sets of pants and sweater. However, she could have chosen something more becoming, just in case. That she hadn't, she now acknowledged, was a childish refusal to admit the appearance was important. Seeing the others—a bearded gentleman in a fine Harris tweed suit; a famous movie star, whose name Norah knew as well as her own and couldn't at this moment remember, in sequins from neck to knees; another woman, not so famous but equally glamorous, in high-necked, long-sleeved, and bare-backed black— Norah wished she'd been a little less intransigent.

"You're next, Lieutenant."

The assistant led her out into the lights and turned her over to Randall Tye. Literally. She was blinded by the brilliance so that Tye had to take her by the hand and lead her to her chair and put her into it. She looked out, but if there was a studio audience, she couldn't see it. Tye's voice as he introduced her sounded far off. The applause shocked her. So there were people out there. That helped. It was something to hang on to. Norah wasn't unaccustomed to making public appearances, addressing small groups. Forget the unseen, uncounted millions at home and concentrate on the people here, she told herself. She folded her hands in her lap and clenched them tightly. After a while what Randall Tye was saying began to get through to her.

He was giving a brief and laudatory account of her time on the force. He included her marriage to Captain Joseph Antony Capretto, his death, her brief leave of absence, and then her return. At the end, the audience broke into cordial applause.

Norah flushed. She couldn't help but be pleased.

"Currently, Lieutenant Mulcahaney heads the investigation into the death of Gilda Valente. It's a fascinating case. I'm sure you've all heard and read about it. Mrs. Valente was socially prominent, served on the board of several charities. Her husband, Dario Valente, is reputed to be high in the ranks of organized crime. She was drowned in her own rooftop swimming pool."

"Just a minute, Mr. Tye." Norah found her voice at last. It was shaky but she went ahead. "We made an agreement, if you recall. I told you before coming on the show that I was not at liberty to discuss a current case."

"Right." Tye smiled genially, not at all disturbed. "The facts I'm presenting are generally known. I'm repeating what's already been reported and discussed in the newspapers and on the television news. I'm not looking for a 'scoop.' " He smiled reassuringly. "My point is that in this investigation you are dealing directly with underworld figures."

"Are you suggesting that Mr. Valente is not entitled to a full and thorough investigation into the death of his wife because of who or what he is alleged to be?"

"No, of course not. What I mean . . ."

"We all accept that an accused person is entitled to the best possible defense. In the same way, every victim, regardless of life style, is entitled to justice."

"Are you reading me a lecture on morality and the law, Lieutenant?" The smile disappeared from the TV host's face. His craggy brow lowered.

"I wouldn't think of it. I'm only telling you that I'm on the side of the victim. Every police officer is. I believe that the justice system is created to protect and avenge the victim and that we are losing sight of that purpose. When we see a victim, each one of us should be thinking—it could have been me."

Applause. It started in scattered sections of the auditorium and spread. It surprised Norah; for a moment she had forgotten where she was. She flushed under the makeup. It made Randall Tye genial again.

"Is that what *you* think when you approach a suspect, Lieutenant?" he asked. "When you approach a suspect, when you go out to make an arrest, do you think that you might become a victim?"

For a long moment Norah remained silent. "Are you asking me if I'm afraid?"

There was a sharp intake of breath from the studio audience. Randall Tye himself edged forward.

"The answer is—yes, I certainly am."

A soft sigh was followed by a ripple of nervous laughter.

"Every police officer knows that he could get blown away any day, any time, any place. If he's not scared, he doesn't understand the job."

"That's right, of course . . ."

"Of course, Mr. Tye?" Norah raised her eyebrows. "My husband was killed in a parking lot when he interrupted a rape. The perpetrators ran over him with their car, crushing his spine. He was caught by the undercarriage and his body dragged six blocks before they knew or cared. Then they abandoned him and fled. And he wasn't even answering a complaint; he just happened to hear a woman scream."

"I'm sorry."

But Norah was wound up. "Do you know what the most potentially dangerous situation a police officer faces is, Mr. Tye? Not a shootout or a car chase; not going undercover or making a drug buy; it's answering a domestic dispute complaint. That's what sends a cold chill through a cop. He doesn't know what's in store. Will it be just a yelling match between husband and wife? Or will he have to deal with an emotionally disturbed person, armed and a danger to himself as well as to others?"

Norah thought of the recent predicament of Detective Gary Reissig, a man for whom she'd once cared and whom she'd come close to marrying. Gary had answered such a call and been confronted by a father holding his two little girls hostage. Gary's action had saved the children but resulted in the father's turning the gun on himself and blowing his brains out. Then Gary had to justify himself before Internal Affairs. No use going into that, she thought.

"These domestic complaints aren't answered by the brass, not even by a lieutenant or sergeant—the department is very short of sergeants these days. No, it's your ordinary RMP, radio motor patrol officer, the workhorse of the department, who responds and puts his life on the line *three or four times a night.*" Norah raised her chin; her dark blue eyes flashed; her voice rang out. "He doesn't get his picture in the paper. He doesn't get invited to appear on your show. But he's the hero."

The applause this time broke out in one spontaneous prolonged demonstration. After a camera sweep of the audience, the control room went to the commercial. The network switchboard lit up.

After the break, the man in Harris tweed was the next guest; the movie star in sequins followed. Norah, dazed, didn't register a word that was said. Then suddenly, it was over and she was surrounded by the other guests, by the staff—the surprised staff. She was called away to take a phone call from Chief Deland. After him, she spoke to Jim Felix. Then there were other calls from people she didn't know. She wanted to respond to them too.

"It's not required," a beaming Randall Tye assured her. "They don't expect to speak to you personally. If you did get on the phone, they wouldn't know what to say."

"My friends . . ."

"Your friends will call you at home. In any case, the operators keep a record—when the caller is willing to give his name. You'll get a copy and you can respond if you feel you want to."

Norah nodded. She was starting to come down from the high of the experience. Reaction was setting in.

"So what do you say we go out, get a bite, and relax?" Tye suggested.

She was hungry, she realized. She was also very tired. "Thanks, but all I really want is to go home."

"Nothing fancy," Tye promised. "There's a little place around the corner. They'll give us a booth in the back. We'll order a steak, have a couple of beers, and that's it."

"Well . . ."

In the lobby of the Valente building when she'd first met Randall Tye, he'd been one of a group of reporters. On the show, she'd been too dazed and bedazzled to take him in. She did so now and where she had wavered between ugly and handsome, she now settled for the latter, very definitely. He was in his early forties and he didn't make the mistake of trying to look younger. On the contrary, he made the most of every line and every crease to suggest a virile maturity. His hair was dark blonde and wavy, his face aquiline. He kept himself slim. He dressed well; none of this coat sweater over an open-necked shirt affectation. He made no pretense of being other than suave, charming, a man of the world. He was good at his job and didn't need a free ride on his looks, yet he used his looks. At a period when newsmen were being shuffled like cards by management, Randall Tye's value was constantly rising.

"What do you say? You've got to eat."

"Okay."

The congratulations continued into Monday and Norah enjoyed them. At first. The calls that reached her at the office were mostly calls from the media requesting interviews, suggesting appearances on other shows. She said no firmly to each. She wished she could just walk away as she had at the studio. She couldn't tell the operator to say she was out because she might miss something important. She sighed as the phone rang again.

"It's Randall, Norah. How are you?"

"Overwhelmed."

"You were a big hit Saturday."

"I don't know why."

"Because you said what you meant. So what I want to know is—will you come back and do it again?"

"Randall, I've had half a dozen offers and I don't want any of them. Honestly, I can't go through it another time. Besides, I've spoken my piece. I've had my fifteen minutes of fame. I can't deny I enjoyed it, but it's over."

"You're going to get a lot more than fifteen minutes."

"I hope not. I have work that's not getting done. I'm sorry."

"Have dinner with me tonight."

"I'm not going to change my mind," she warned.

"I won't ask you to. Just dinner. I'll pick you up at your place at eight." He hung up before she could argue anymore.

But not all reaction was favorable. Criticism trickled through the praise. Lieutenant Mulcahaney was too simplistic, some said. Under the guise of compassion for the victim, she prejudged. She had the mentality of a storm trooper. She was taking a giant step backward to the bad old days of prejudice and racial bias.

Norah was hurt, bewildered, then finally indignant. How could anyone work racial bias into what she'd said?

Milo Vanderberg called a press conference. The gist of his verbose statement:

Lieutenant Mulcahaney's tribute to the dedication and courage of the ordinary cop on the Randall Tye show Saturday night was false and misleading. Her response and that of the New York Police Department, or rather the lack of it, to the complaint of my client, Carl Pesrow, negates everything she said. Carl Pesrow is a victim. Carl Pesrow was shot on a city street, but the lieutenant is not doing anything about it. She is neither investigating in good faith nor offering Mr. Pesrow the protection to which he is entitled, while the acknowledged perpetrator, Stefanie Altman, is free on bail.

The kicker:

We intend to sue Lieutenant Mulcahaney and the NYPD for one million dollars for pain, anxiety, and the deprivation of Carl Pesrow's constitutional rights.

"What does that mean?" Norah demanded as she stormed in to Manny Jacoby.

"Anything they want it to mean." He shrugged. "The PC and the chief aren't worried. They want you to accept the invitations you've been getting from the various shows. They want you right up front where the public can see you."

"I don't think it's a good idea, Captain. I think my appearance on the Randall Tye show is what put this idea into Vanderberg's head."

"Neither the PC nor Chief Deland feel that way. They like how you handled yourself. They still see it as good PR. They realize you're carrying a heavy load, so . . ."

Norah held her breath.

"So if you need additional help, we'll find it for you. Somehow."

Norah exhaled. She had been afraid that in order to accommodate the PR duty she might be relieved of one, if not both, cases.

"Thanks, Captain."

"Don't thank me. It wasn't my decision." Jacoby's pudgy face was set in folds of disapproval. "Oh, here." He handed her a page torn from his own appointment pad. "You're on the *Phil Donahue Show* today. They want you at that address."

She stared at the paper. "This afternoon?"

"You have a problem with that, Lieutenant?"

"Yes, sir, I do. The grand jury hearing of the Altman case is scheduled for this afternoon. As the arresting officer, Wyler is on the list to give evidence. I wanted to review with him . . ."

"It's been postponed.

"The hearing? I didn't know."

"It was decided this morning. The DA agreed we should try to locate the missing witness."

"Oh." She looked at Jacoby and broke out into a big grin. It had been his doing, of course. "Thanks, Captain."

In her office, the phone was ringing. Another secretary calling for another producer, another reporter wanting an interview, neither of which she could now refuse, she thought as she picked up the receiver.

"You don't know me, Lieutenant. I saw you on the Randall Tye show Saturday night."

The voice was a woman's—light, not only young but timid.

"I tried to reach you at the station but the calls were backed up and by the time it was my turn, you had left."

"I'm sorry. What can I do for you?"

"I have information. Information that I believe would interest you."

Nervous too, Norah thought, very nervous. "Can you give me an idea of what it's about?"

"Oh. It's about Gilda Valente."

About her, not about her death, Norah registered. "I'd be interested in anything you can tell me. What's your name?"

"Imogene."

Norah hesitated and decided not to press. "Where can we meet?"

Apparently she had thought that out because she answered promptly. "Do you skate, Lieutenant?"

"Skate? Not very well."

"The Wollman Rink at one this afternoon." She hung up.

So, Norah thought as she leaned back in her chair, the television appearance had resulted in the threat of a lawsuit and a lead in the Valente case. The pluses might outweigh the minuses, after all.

CHAPTER NINE

The sun was shining in a cloudless sky as Norah Mulcahaney left the Eighty-second Street station house and headed for the park. The temperature had been slowly rising since morning and had reached a balmy thirty-two degrees for the first time since the paralyzing blizzard a week ago. She entered Central Park at Seventy-ninth and headed downtown toward the Wollman Rink, which, after years of political boondoggling, had finally been reconstructed by the effort of private enterprise and was back in operation. Though all that was left of the snow on city streets was grimy gray patches, out here it still lay in vast unbroken stretches across fields and lawns and rocky outcroppings. The bare tree limbs were crystalline against the blue sky. The branches of pines were heavily laden as though decorated for Christmas.

It should have been easy to lose herself, to make believe at least for the length of her walk that she was far away in the country, to set aside her problems. But she couldn't. According to the statistics released by the FBI and the State of New York, the incidence of homicide and felonies in the city were both up, but the rise in murders was dramatic. In twenty-one precincts, murders showed a 50 percent increase over the preceding year. Though the rise in Norah's Fourth Zone was not that high, it was still a matter of grave concern. For two homicides, both "mysteries," to occur within hours of each other within the zone put a heavy burden on the squad. "Mysteries" in police parlance meant exactly that—cases that did not readily lend themselves to obvious and quick solutions.

The Altman case was a mystery because Stefanie Altman was both victim and perpetrator; because the circumstances were unclear; because the stories of Altman and Pesrow conflicted and one of them had to be lying, maybe both. If indeed a third man was involved he might be able to give the answer. According to Wyler's reports he'd tried the Acme Agency Pesrow had mentioned, but hadn't turned up any leads. She scribbled a note for him: *Try the carpet warehouse.*

As for the Valente case, no trace of drugs or alcohol had been found in Gilda Valente's body, thus eliminating the slight possibility that the drowning was an accident. Norah felt she could rule out suicide too. The woman was a strong swimmer. If she'd wanted to die by drowning she might do so in the ocean by going out so far that she had no strength to get back, but not in her own pool. And there was, of course, the damp bath towel on the lounge chair beside the pool. The lab analysis hadn't come in yet. Until it did, the towel was merely suggestive. Norah sighed. Maybe the woman she was going to meet would provide a lead.

Faint strains of Christmas carols wafted over the snowy landscape as Norah climbed over the last knoll to the skating rink. At the crest, she paused to enjoy the colorful scene below. Music filled the air. Skaters swirled or labored, according to their skills, but everywhere there were smiles and laughter. The rink was more crowded than Norah had expected on a weekday. There were elderly couples who crossed arms and waltzed serenely; mothers with under–school-aged children clutching at their knees as they wobbled on the ice. There were also older boys and girls who should have been in school and adults who should have been working. Well, it was a beautiful day, Norah thought, and these people knew how to set aside responsibilities and get out and enjoy it. She wished she could do the same, but it simply wasn't in her. She had used to think of herself as dedicated, now she was beginning to wonder if she wasn't in a rut. Maybe she was missing something important by letting the special moments life offered slip by.

She walked out on the terrace overlooking the rink and watched the skaters glide by, scrutinizing each one. She had no idea whom she was looking for, or even exactly where the meeting was to take place. The caller would know her, of course, since she'd seen her on the show. All she had to do was stand there and wait to be approached. Ten minutes went by, fifteen. The music segued from carols to waltzes, and back again. It occurred to Norah that the caller had asked if she could skate. Was she expected to get out there on the ice? Well, why not?

When she was a little girl, before her mother's death changed everything, Norah had learned to skate. She hadn't been bad either. That was a long time ago, she thought as she laced up the rented boots, but it was supposed to be one of those skills one never forgot. She managed to get across the wooden planking from the bench to the ice with reasonable steadiness, but her satisfaction was premature. She took three steps on the ice and her ankles turned and she went down—hard.

Two boys stifled their laughter and came forward politely.

"Help you, ma'am?"

They set her on her feet and skated off.

The meeting place was indeed shrewdly selected, Norah thought as she clung to the rail. The witness could say what she had to say and be gone before Norah could make a move. However, except for the two boys, nobody came near her. As she made her awkward way around the rink, nobody spoke to her. Her confidence grew, some of her skill returned till she was able to let go the bar and move without support. Yet as she became more proficient, Norah's hope that her informant would appear decreased. What had gone wrong?

It was a quarter of two and the *Phil Donahue Show* aired at four, so once more around and she'd have to call it quits, Norah thought, surprised at the extent of her disappointment, surprised at how much she'd been counting on this interview. Actually, she'd been looking not so much for specific information as for guidance in the direction she should take. There were several possibilities, she mused as she glided, almost gracefully, in time to the music. One: the spouse. The spouse was always the primary suspect, but in this instance the marriage was universally acknowledged to have been happy. Also, Dario Valente had a powerful alibi. On the other hand, there was no need for him to have committed the act himself; he could have ordered it. Two: an inside job. The security arrangements made that likely. The *capo* trusted his people, but one of them could have turned traitor, could have been seduced by a rival organization. But if a rival gang was behind Gilda Valente's death, wouldn't they want Valente to know?

Skating in long, rhythmic strides and absorbed in her thoughts, Norah was startled to hear a break in the music and her name announced over the loudspeakers.

"Lieutenant Mulcahaney, please come to the park ranger station."

Norah left the ice and still on skates strode briskly over the planked flooring to a small, white-shingled hut and went inside.

"Lieutenant Mulcahaney? We have an urgent telephone call for you." The ranger handed her the receiver.

"It's Ferdi Arenas, Lieutenant. I'm at 101A West Ninety-fifth Street. A woman jumped or fell or was pushed from a fifth-story window. She had your name on a pad and two numbers with it: one for the Liberty Network and the other for the squad."

Norah took a deep, deep breath and slowly exhaled. "I'm on my way."

The victim lay on the pavement, arms and legs at unnatural angles like a doll assembled by someone unfamiliar with the human anatomy. The back of her head was a mass of blood and fragmented bone, but miraculously her features hadn't caved in. She had been pretty, Norah thought: in her late twenties, with small, neat features, short dark hair, and hazel eyes that were wide open in the full realization of how it was all going to end. She'd landed in front of a small antique shop. Held back by the RMPs, a group of her neighbors stared in stunned silence. Five floors above, curtains billowed in an open window.

Arenas met Norah when she arrived.

"Anybody see it happen?" she asked.

He shook his head. "The owner of the shop heard her hit. He was in the back uncrating some new acquisitions. He couldn't identify the sound but it brought him running. After he got through being sick, he called in." Arenas consulted his notebook. "The call was logged at 12:36 hours."

Taking into account the shop owner's reaction that would move it up a few minutes. Just about the time she might have been expected to be leaving for the Wollman Rink, Norah thought.

"Let's go up."

There was no elevator, so they walked. Norah expected the tenants to come out to see what was going on, even to ask questions. Curiosity vanquished horror every time. But no one so much as put his head out.

"Where is everybody?"

"Most of them work during the day," Ferdi told her.

They said no more till they reached the apartment. It was a floor-through consisting of living room, dining room, and two bedrooms. One bedroom was obviously in use and the other not. Though the rooms were small, it was still a lot of space by present city standards.

"Was she married?" Norah asked.

"No."

"Did she have a roommate?"

"Lived alone. No boyfriend. No parties. Kept to herself, the super says."

"A woman called me at the squad this morning. Said

she had information about Gilda Valente and arranged to meet me at the Wollman Rink at one. She never showed." Norah paused. "She didn't give me her name, just said Imogene."

"Imogene Davies." Again Arenas consulted his note-book. "Age twenty-four. Used to work at Le Salon as a hairdresser."

"Used to?"

"Got fired—the super isn't sure how long ago."

That could be the connection, Norah thought. Women tend to confide in their hairdressers, tell them things they wouldn't dream of even hinting about to their nearest and dearest friends or family.

"If she called you and made a date to meet you, Lieutenant, she wasn't likely to have had suicide on her mind."

"It wouldn't seem so." She walked over to the open window. The sill outside was broad, unusually so, and waist high. Imogene Davies would have had to be leaning way out for the fall to have been accidental. Way, way out.

That left murder.

What did Imogene Davies know that got her killed?

As Norah and Ferdi Arenas went through the apartment together, not only searching for indications of what might have happened, but also to learn something about the young woman who had lived there, her character and life style, both got the feeling that someone had gone through it before them. Not knowing the victim's habits or what valuables she'd had, it was hard to tell whether anything had been disturbed, impossible to know what might be missing. One thing was apparent, however: Imogene Davies had been house proud. Everything was polished to mirrorlike perfection. Not a chair was out of line. If anyone had tossed the place ahead of them he had been remarkably meticulous, but he had missed on the pillows. Of a matching pair embroidered with the tree-of-life pattern and set precisely at each end of a deep-blue velvet sofa, one was upside down.

Norah checked her watch: two-twenty-five. She must

leave for the studio. Now. But she lingered. From an end table she picked up a framed photograph. The slightly blurred focus and the carelessness of the pose suggested it was an enlargement from a snapshot. Taken outdoors on a spring day, in the park—Norah recognized the Bow Bridge and the western skyline—it showed two young women and a man, arms linked, laughing, the wind ruffling their hair. The girl on the right was the one Norah had just seen on the pavement below—Imogene Davies. The other was Gilda Valente. The man was blonde, handsome, blue eyes, younger than either woman. She passed the photograph over to Ferdi.

"Find out who the man is. Have copies made of the photo and leave a couple on my desk so I can show Valente."

Still she didn't go.

"We don't know what we're looking for so listen to everything. Oh, hell, Ferdi, you know what to do. Go ahead and do it." Norah walked out. But she came right back.

"Find out if Davies was ever married or if she ever had a roommate. This place is much too big for a single woman."

"Yes, Lieutenant."

"You'll show the photo to the neighbors while you're at it, of course."

"Of course, Lieutenant." He managed not to smile.

Ferdi knew that neither Norah's instructions nor her reluctance to leave had anything to do with a lack of trust in his ability. They had been together too many years, had supported each other through too many professional and personal crises for him to have any doubts. But he had never seen her so edgy.

"Well, if you need me you know where I am."

"Where?" Ferdi asked.

"On another one of those dumb shows, where else?" she said in frustration. She scribbled the number for him on a slip of paper. This time when she closed the door, she didn't open it again.

With Norah gone, Arenas went over the apartment

once more. He found nothing more of interest. The contents of the closets appeared to have been disturbed, or it was possible that Imogene Davies's neatness didn't extend to what was out of sight. Nonetheless, he called for the fingerprint detectives. By the time they arrived, did their work, and left, it was after five. The neighbors would be getting back from work.

It was a small building. Tenants knew each other well enough to exchange greetings. Though curious about each other, they were loath to ask questions so that they in turn would not be required to give answers. In big cities, respect for privacy was an obsession. Observations were made and passed on and then conclusions drawn at second or even third hand. Surprising how often even the most off-the-mark conjecture held some grain of fact at the core. Listen to everything, Norah had said, and Arenas intended to do just that. He started with the dead girl's next-door neighbor. The nameplate on the door read: E. Youngblood.

Ms. Youngblood was fiftyish, gray-haired, plump. As she edged open the door and peered at Arenas through the slit permitted by the length of the door chain, he was aware of bright eyes, pursed lips, and a soft, cushiony bosom upon which the black ribbon of her glasses was draped like military braid.

Arenas identified himself. "I'd like to talk to you for a few moments about the young woman next door."

"Oh, yes, I heard. A terrible thing. Poor child. Yes, come in." It took several moments for her to remove the chain and let him in.

The apartment was surprising. Though much smaller than the other, it was beautifully furnished. Ferdi was no expert, but he knew instinctively he was looking at genuine antiques and that the carpets were exceptionally fine Orientals. Ms. Youngblood's quite evident pride confirmed his assessment.

"May I ask exactly what you heard and from whom?"

Ms. Youngblood sighed. "I heard the poor child is dead. The super, Mr. Max, told me as I came in. It seems she fell or jumped . . ." Sighing, she spread her hands in a gesture of futility and regret.

"What do you think happened?"

"I don't know. I couldn't say."

"Did you notice any change in Ms. Davies's behavior recently?"

"I didn't know her that well. I didn't see her that often. We'd pass each other going in and out, say hello, remark on the weather—that kind of thing." She paused, considering. "She did seem somewhat down, I must say, in the past two or three weeks. Maybe longer than that. I heard she was fired from her job and was having financial problems."

"Is that so?"

"I understand she was behind in the rent and was looking for another roommate to help defray expenses. She wasn't having much success, apparently. The agency through which she got the last one didn't want to deal with her anymore."

"Why was that?"

Suddenly, Ms. Youngblood decided she'd gone too far. The color rose in her colorless face. "I don't know. I'm sorry. I'm repeating what I heard and I have no way of knowing if it's true or not." She was quick to dissociate herself, to avoid involvement, no matter how limited.

"From whom did you hear it?"

"I'm not even sure of that. I can't remember."

No use pressing, Ferdi thought. Even if she knew, it was apparent she'd made up her mind not to tell. "What was the name of the previous roommate?"

"I'm sorry. It's almost six months since she left."

Arenas decided to drop it. He had, in fact, already garnered more than he'd expected. He would show her the photograph, though. "This is Ms. Davies, of course. Do you recognize the other two?"

Ms. Youngblood looked at the picture closely. For a long time. "Yes, that's Imogene," she admitted almost reluctantly. There was another pause. "I don't know the other two. I don't recall ever having seen either one. I wish

I could be more helpful, Sergeant, but I really have no more time. I have a dinner engagement. I should have left long since." She lacked her earlier composure. From flushed she'd turned white again, whiter than when she'd first opened the door to Arenas.

"I apologize for the inconvenience, ma'am. You've been very helpful." As he spoke, she was backing him to the door and into the hall. Before he could finish, it was closed in his face.

Ms. E. Youngblood, while not particularly forthcoming, had been pleasant enough, Ferdi thought. Until he showed her the photograph. Something in it had frightened her. Scared her stiff.

CHAPTER
TEN

Simon Wyler was outraged and appalled not just by Milo Vanderberg's threat to sue on behalf of his client, but by the meek, temporizing response from the PC's office. Couldn't anybody besides him and the lieut see that the case was upside down, the roles reversed? Maybe the idea was to avoid dignifying the charge? Still, it wasn't right. Who were the guys in the white hats anyway?

In the years since Wyler had transferred from Midtown South, he had learned that Lieutenant Mulcahaney took the department guidelines regarding the use of physical force very seriously. She put a premium on brains and it wasn't because she couldn't handle herself, but because she was too smart to get into situations where force was the only solution. She expected her people to be just as smart. It suited Wyler; violence was not his style. He started taking courses at John Jay College. In his personal life, he selected his girlfriends on the basis not merely of looks but of his own expanding interests. Kaja was an actress; with her he went to the theater and the opera. Annie was an athlete; they attended the basketball games (she'd played center on a girls' interscholastic team). Millicent was a class A tennis player and expert skier. Lola—Lola was none of the above and it didn't matter. When Lola came along everything changed. She was what Simon

Wyler had been searching for and so was the job at the Fourth. Simon saw the Altman case as his opportunity to prove his worth. He was determined to clear it. The lieut was set on finding the third alleged mugger, but he'd spent the whole damn week on it and got nowhere. It was time to try something else.

To understand what had happened on the stoop on Seventy-sixth Street the night of the blizzard, what Stefanie Altman had done and why, he had to learn more about her, Wyler decided. A plain girl, with little future in her hometown, she'd come to New York to make something of her life. Untrained, with no particular talent and no marketable skill beyond typing, she had on the basis of willingness and diligence managed to get a job as a receptionist at a small but prestigious advertising agency. It was not what she wanted. She tried again, four times in all—as a salesgirl at Bonwit's, a typist and file clerk at IBM, a secretary at Williston and Coe, Real Estate. In none of these positions did she perform with particular distinction or find the inner satisfaction she sought. It was the bookshop that fulfilled Stefie Altman. Through it she earned a living, developed confidence, made friends. It even got her Timothy Kampel.

Monday night, Wyler met Kampel at the Met in the Grand Tier Restaurant where he moonlighted as a waiter. The dinner hour was over. The tables had been cleared and reset for the entr'acte. In about twenty minutes the great gold curtain would come down on the first act of *Tosca* and the audience would rush out of the concert hall and up the broad, red-carpeted stairs, under the snowflake chandeliers for a glass of champagne, a pastry, even a sandwich and coffee. Until then, the place was empty. Tim Kampel led the detective to a table overlooking the small park in front of the Vivian Beaumont theater. In all the performances Wyler had attended with his opera expert, Kaja, they had never been able to afford to come in here and sit down like this.

"Why do you keep picking on Stefie?" Kampel demanded. "She had to shoot to protect herself. If she'd gone ahead and let those guys rape her, maybe kill her, then you would have had your evidence. Then you'd be satisfied, I suppose."

Wyler agreed, even shared his indignation, but that was no way to extract information. "We know that Ms. Altman's shop was broken into four times in the last three months. Understandably, that would make her nervous. Perhaps it would cause her to overreact to the approach of the three men."

"Look, I was with her just before it happened. I picked her up at the shop and offered to walk her all the way home, but she said no. So I left her at Columbus. She was calm, relaxed, at ease. She was not expecting or looking for trouble. But those guys sure were. Don't tell me they followed her up Columbus, turned the corner of her block, and ran to catch up with her just to ask directions to the nearest subway. Don't tell me you believe that. I know better and so do you."

"They were laughing," Wyler reminded him. "There are neighbors who heard the laughter in the street just before the gunshots."

"They were drunk, for God's sake! They were lurching around in the snow laughing in anticipation of the fun they were going to have with Stefie. Their laughter terrorized her! She's the victim. Have you forgotten that? Why are you wasting time investigating her? Why don't you investigate Beech? I'll bet he's got a criminal record as long as my arm." In a burst of indignation Kampel extended an arm. "Both arms." He held out the other.

"As a matter of fact, Mr. Kampel, he doesn't," Wyler told him.

"Oh. So, are you going to stop at that?"

"We haven't stopped. We already know that Frank Beech had a very sketchy work history. He held a variety of jobs, none of them for very long. In fact, he was out of work more often than not. He seemed to hold a job just long enough to become eligible for unemployment compensation and then find one when benefits ran out. At the time of the incident, Frank Beech was out of work and out of benefits."

"There you are; he was looking for somebody to hit on. It was a bad night; the street was deserted; Stefie was alone—the perfect victim."

Wyler didn't comment.

"How much money did Beech have in his pocket?" Kampel demanded. "Suppose they'd drunk up all their funds, the three of them, and they were looking not for directions to get home, but for money to put in the turnstile or even to go on drinking?"

"Pesrow says they had money to get home."

"What would you expect him to say?" Kampel retorted. "I want to ask you something, Detective Wyler. Recently, there were two similar cases. Two black men—one a subway token clerk and the other a liquor store owner. Each shot his would-be assailant. The district attorney didn't bring charges against either one."

"What's your point?"

"Why is the district attorney so determined to convict Stefie? He isn't prosecuting, he's persecuting her. Why?"

"I suppose because he believes he has a case."

"What do you believe?"

"It doesn't matter what I believe, Mr. Kampel. My job is to gather evidence."

Norah Mulcahaney's second television appearance turned out to be much less of an ordeal than her first on *People in the News*. The activity before airtime didn't seem so frenetic. The bright lights were not so dazzling. Her pulse quickened at the countdown to airtime; her heart pounded, but it was pleasurable. All at once, she felt proud to have been chosen to speak for the department.

Then suddenly, it was over. She was warmly congratulated by the host, the producer, the director. Calls were coming in, the preponderance favorable, she was told. Of course, there were always the kooks; you had to expect that. Expressions of mutual regard were exchanged, and then she was alone. She had come in her own car and now as she went around to the parking lot she felt let down and at loose ends.

She returned to the station house. Nobody said much to her as she walked past the duty desk. In the squad room, nobody mentioned the show. Naturally, nobody had seen it. Who had time to watch television in the middle of the afternoon? Just the same, Norah was disappointed. She checked her calls, went through the accumulated forms and memos on her desk. There was nothing from Wyler or from Ferdi. Too soon, she thought, much too soon. So why not go home, soak in a hot tub, and make it an early night? Then she remembered the date with Randall Tye. She could cancel. On the other hand, she could use a change of pace.

A change of pace was what she got. Randall Tye gave her a night on the town. Norah wasn't prepared for it. She certainly wasn't dressed for it. When she learned they were going to Le Cirque for dinner, she wanted to change. Tye told her she couldn't look more beautiful. He made her almost believe him. From the muted elegance of the famous restaurant with its red slip-covered banquettes they went on to the newly refurbished and reopened Rainbow Room. They joined a private party at which Tye had promised to put in an appearance. Finally, they wound up the evening to the thundering beat and laser display of The Tunnel. Everywhere Randall Tye was fussed over, somehow a table magically appeared for him in the best location. Norah was greeted politely because she was with him. That wasn't good enough for Tye. He made a point of telling each maître d' and the guests who stopped by *who* she was. She couldn't help but be gratified by the instant change in attitude.

Norah had never been in such places before. She started off feeling out of her element and ended up having a wonderful time. She forgot about being tired. It was 1:00 A.M. before she reluctantly called it a night.

Tye didn't argue. He took her straight home as soon as she asked.

"I don't suppose you're going to invite me in," he said as they stood outside her door.

"For you, it's the shank of the evening, but it's way past my bedtime. It was wonderful, Randall. I had the best time I've had in years. Thank you."

"I'm glad." He hesitated. "I'll call you in the morning."

Timothy Kampel's accusation that Wyler had spent all his time probing Stefanie Altman's past and her motive for shooting Frank Beech stung. He couldn't admit to Kampel that the reason he had put so much time in on her was that he hoped to find something, some tangible evidence to support her version of what had happened. He was loath to admit it to himself. He had hinted of his feelings to the lieut and she'd warned him against taking sides—in essence, prejudging. Actually, it wasn't taking sides, it was more like a hunch. He believed in Stefie Altman's innocence. Nothing wrong with that. But maybe he'd been going about proving it in the wrong way. Maybe it was Frank Beech's past he should be digging into.

So early Tuesday morning, Wyler took the ferry to Staten Island.

Frank Beech had lived with his mother and father in a two-story frame house near one of the marinas. The father, Fred Beech, was a fisherman. He owned a small boat and for most of the year he took out day-trippers. In the off-season, which was now, he went out on his own. So he wasn't home when Simon Wyler came calling. But Mrs. Beech was. She seemed a decent woman, more bewildered over the death of her son than grieving. Her instinct was to defend him and protect his reputation. What else could he have expected? Wyler thought.

"Frank was a good boy," Doris Beech kept repeating. She was a stout woman in a flowered housedress that didn't quite cover knobby white knees showing over the tops of her knee-high nylons. "He was a good boy. A little wild sometimes maybe, like most boys."

"Wild? In what way?" Wyler asked.

"Well, not wild exactly. Not part of a gang, or using

drugs, or anything like that, thank God. He was popular. With the girls. They liked him. Know what I mean?" She shrugged. "It wasn't Frank's fault if the girls liked him, was it?"

Wyler got the drift, but he had to be careful how he drew the facts from her. It was like pulling a thread from fabric. He must take great care not to break it.

"Did Frank ever get a girl into trouble?" He didn't know how else to put it, but he made sure not to indicate blame, if anything to suggest sympathy.

"Things are different nowadays," Mrs. Beech pointed out. "Nowadays, girls know what they're doing. Girls don't get *into trouble* unless they want to."

So there had been an incident, Wyler thought, his senses quickening, at least one. Probably in high school. "Did Frank have a steady girlfriend?" Doris Beech shook her head. "How about at work? Did he date any girls from the job?" Wyler persisted but kept his manner easy.

"Frank had a lot of girlfriends."

"What was the last job he held down, Mrs. Beech?"

"Why do you want to know? What's all this got to do with what happened?"

"I can't say till I get the answers, ma'am. I asked the same questions about Ms. Altman," he assured her.

Doris Beech had been sitting at the kitchen table; now, all at once, she got up on her swollen legs. "Want a beer?"

"No, thanks."

She went to the refrigerator and pulled out a cold can and with practiced thumb and forefinger pulled off the tab and poured. She took a long, greedy swallow. She was like a chain-smoker getting his first lung-filling drag in the morning. "He worked in the mail room. I don't remember the name of the company."

She couldn't name any of the companies Frank Beech had worked for in the last couple of years. "He moved around a lot. He was still young, restless. Why should he shut himself up from nine to five during the best years of his life? There was plenty of time for him to settle down."

And that, at last, brought tears to her rheumy eyes. So she solaced herself with another draught.

"What Frank wanted was to be a pilot. He was trying to get into a training program run by the National Guard. I don't know the details, only that there was a long waiting list. So meantime, his father was on him to help out on the boat, summers at least, when business is real heavy. But Frank wasn't into fishing."

The old story of the chasm between generations, Wyler thought. Economic circumstances didn't seem to have anything to do with it. The young adult resided in his parents' house like a stranger and kept the details of his real existence hidden. And the parents learned not to ask for fear of even appearing to pry. Wyler was sure he would get more about Frank from the neighbors, and as for past employment—that information would be readily available at the local Social Security office. He thanked Doris Beech and left her pouring out her second beer.

Wyler grabbed a hamburger and made it to the Social Security office in the early afternoon. The supervisor was young, with smooth, coffee-colored skin, small neat features under a frizz of dark curls. She was too pretty to be bearing the weight of the world on her shoulders, Wyler thought, and gave her his most engaging smile and then told her exactly what he needed and why he needed it. The combination worked. Jeannie Dulac stopped scowling and led him to her office, where she punched up Frank Beech's work record on the computer terminal.

Williston and Coe, Real Estate. The name jumped at Wyler. Beech had worked there from July to early December of the previous year. He didn't need to consult his notebook to recall that Stefanie Altman had also worked there, but he had to make absolutely sure that both had been there at the same time. As he fumbled nervously through the pages, his anxiety grew. Yes. His heart sank. Yes, their periods of employment overlapped. Altman worked as a secretary in the executive offices and Beech in the mail room, but who would believe they had never met, had no knowledge of each other?

It shook Wyler badly. He almost wished he hadn't found out, but since he had—he had no choice but to follow up on it.

CHAPTER
ELEVEN

After leaving Ms. E. Youngblood, Imogene Davies's next-door neighbor, Sergeant Fernando Arenas immediately applied to the building superintendent. He had not only the name of the dead woman's ex-roommate, but her forwarding address. Pleased with the progress, Ferdi called home and told Concepción to put dinner on the table.

Tuesday brought another of the bright, crisp, frigid mornings they'd had since the storm. Ferdi took the subway from his apartment in Forest Hills, got off at the first stop in Manhattan, and walked to Sixty-fifth between Madison and Park Avenues. The building was a small, elegant, Georgian-style mansion subdivided into apartments of "quiet distinction," as they say in the real estate ads. There was no doorman, but by what Ferdi could see through the glass panel—black marble floor with brass inlay and a small crystal chandelier—it was not a matter of economy. He found the name he wanted and pressed the bell beside it. He was leaning forward to announce himself when the door's buzzer sounded and the lock was released.

He entered, located the self-service elevator at the rear, and rode up to the third floor. There were two facing doors in the narrow vestibule. Again he was anticipated and the door to his left was opened.

She was a robust, large-bosomed redhead clutching at a flowered kimono. Her face was round, somewhat swollen; her tangled curls in need of combing; her brown, velvety eyes bleary with sleep seeds at the corners.

She blinked at Ferdi. "I thought you were the laundryman." She spoke with a soft drawl he couldn't quite place.

"No, I'm Sergeant Arenas from the Fourth Division." He showed her his ID. "Sorry to get you up."

"I didn't sleep too well," she admitted, stifling a yawn.

The robe parted enough to reveal a plump, rosy thigh and bare feet surprisingly tiny for her upper endowments.

"Actually, Sergeant, I'm glad you're here," Mary Ruth Rae said. "I was trying to decide what to do. So now you've made the decision for me. Come on in."

The apartment combined the modern with the antique. The walls were stark white without molding or other architectural ornamentation. The floor was highly polished parquet on which several rich, glowing orientals were displayed. Sofa and chairs were a neutral beige and the coffee table was a massive mirrored block. All the rest were fine period pieces, no doubt of their authenticity. The main object, however, the one that claimed immediate attention as well as taking up the most space, was a concert grand piano. Few New York apartments were large enough to accommodate such an instrument.

"Do you play?" Arenas asked.

"No, I sing," Mary Ruth Rae replied. "I used to do gospel and country. Now I'm into opera."

That explained the modulated drawl, Arenas thought; she was trying to get rid of what had once been an asset. "That's quite a switch."

"Not if you've got the voice. And a good coach, of course," the redhead replied. "And you've got to be willing to work."

"I'm sure of that."

"Want some coffee? I'm no good in the morning till I have my first cup."

"I never say no to coffee," Ferdi told her and followed the singer into the kitchen. It was narrow, galley style, with a lavish assortment of pots and pans and utensils hanging from the ceiling. "You must enjoy cooking."

For a moment, the remark seemed to take her by surprise. Then Mary Ruth Rae smiled. "Oh, yes." She unhooked a saucepan and filled it with water from the tap and set it on the large range to boil. She placed a pair of fine china cups on the counter and carefully spooned instant coffee into them. When the water was boiling, she poured and stirred. "Sugar? Milk?"

"Just milk, thank you."

From the huge refrigerator, she handed Ferdi the container. "Help yourself." Then she carried her own cup, black, over to a nook with built-in table and facing bench seats.

Ferdi joined her, stirred his coffee, and waited.

"I suppose you're here about poor Imogene," the redhead sighed. "I heard about it on the radio last night. I couldn't believe it. I was completely devastated. I mean, you never think these terrible things can happen to anyone you actually know."

"I understand you roomed with her."

"I moved out six months ago. We didn't part friends, I'm sorry to say. I haven't seen or spoken to her since."

"You were hesitating about whether or not to get in touch with us. You must have had something on your mind," Ferdi reasoned.

"No, not really. Imo wasn't the easiest person in the world to live with. She had low self-esteem. Also, she was very jealous. I guess one goes with the other. I don't know; I'm not a psychiatrist."

"What was she jealous about?"

The redhead sipped her coffee, then put it down. "She accused me of stealing her boyfriend. The fact is they were on the verge of breaking up before I ever moved in."

Ferdi brought out the photograph he'd taken from Davies's apartment. "Is this him?"

Mary Ruth nodded. "That's Peter. Peter Hines. He's a singer too, so we had a lot in common. Imo resented that. She imagined there was more to it than music and trying to get ahead in the same profession. She got suspicious and nasty. She was cranky at home and she carried her bad temper to work. The ladies who were clients at Le Salon weren't inclined to put up with it. They started asking for other operators, or even going somewhere else. Finally she got fired. Or that's what I heard. I'd moved into this place by then."

Pleasant as the other apartment was, this was in a different class completely, Ferdi thought. "Would you say she was at a very low ebb—fired from her job, behind in her rent? Emotional as she tended to be, was it enough to make her decide to end her own life?"

Mary Ruth frowned. "I don't know. She was certainly moody."

"Yet yesterday morning just a few hours before her death, Imogene Davies called the police and said she had information she wanted to pass on. Did you know that?"

The brown, velvety eyes opened wide. "No. How could I? I told you I haven't seen or spoken to Imogene since I moved out."

"Have you any idea what that information might have been?"

Mary Ruth Rae shook her head.

Once again Arenas referred to the picture. "Do you know the other woman in this photo?"

She nodded. "Mrs. Gilda Valente."

"The information Ms. Davies wanted to pass on concerned Mrs. Valente."

Mary Ruth remained silent.

"The three of them sure look friendly, wouldn't you say?"

"They were—at one time," the redhead replied. "Mrs. Valente was a client of Imogene's. She sent Imo a lot of her high-society friends. Built up a high-powered following for her. Imo introduced her to Peter and Mrs. Valente took an interest in his career. She got him a good voice coach and paid for his lessons. I believe it was as much out of friendship for Imo as for Peter's sake. Mrs. Valente was a patron of the arts. Know what I mean? She helped young people she believed had talent." She paused, gathered her robe around her, and sat up, bosom thrust forward. "Actually, she was helping me too. She was paying for my voice lessons."

"Is that so?

"Rich people do that," Mary Ruth stated. "They subsidize painters, sculptors—all kinds of artists."

"Could that be what Ms. Davies wanted to tell us?"

Mary Ruth Rae shrugged. "It wasn't any secret, not in music circles anyway. Unless she wanted to make more out of the relationship between Peter and Mrs. Valente than there actually was. She might have wanted to make trouble for Peter. I'm sorry to speak ill of the dead, but Imogene was very vindictive."

Having called the police and made the date to meet Norah, Imogene Davies might then have also called Hines and warned him she intended to involve him in Gilda Valente's death, Ferdi thought. Naturally, Hines would have tried to talk her out of it. He could even have gone over to the apartment to try to dissuade her. There would have been an argument. A struggle. And in the course of the struggle . . . No. No struggle, Ferdi decided. It had been a cold day and the window would have been closed. In a struggle, the victim would have crashed through the glass. The window had been open—opened either by the victim to commit suicide, or by the killer.

"Was she vindictive toward you?" Ferdi asked. "You did say she thought you'd stolen her boyfriend. Also, you were benefiting from Mrs. Valente's generosity, as she had earlier. Maybe she wanted to make trouble for you."

The large brown eyes filled. "We were close once and I'd hate to think she'd do a thing like that, but . . ." she sighed. "As I said, she was very mixed up. Almost, what do they call it, schizoid." She sighed again. "Poor, poor Imo."

"Do you know where I can reach Peter Hines?"

"No, I'm sorry. After I moved out, we lost touch."

"I would have thought . . ." Arenas stopped. "Never mind. Your voice coach will surely know."

"We don't have the same coach. Not anymore. I don't know who he's taking from now. Actually, I don't think he's taking from anybody. I heard Mrs. Valente dropped him."

"Why was that?"

The redhead hesitated. She licked her full lips with the first sign of nervousness. "He wasn't fulfilling his promise."

And you could take that a lot of different ways, Ferdi thought.

There was another question he wanted to ask, but he decided it would be good to consult Norah first. He thanked the singer and left. Finding a phone booth on the corner, he dialed the squad. Lieutenant Mulcahaney hadn't come in. He glanced at his watch. After ten. He tried her apartment anyway. She wasn't there either.

By the time Simon Wyler finished at the Social Security office on Staten Island and got back to Manhattan Tuesday afternoon, it was too late to go to Williston and Coe. But on Wednesday morning, he was at the door waiting for the real estate firm to open. The organization was large, occupying several floors of a building on Madison and Sixtieth. Wyler started with the mail room.

Personnel turnover was heavy and constant and Frank Beech had stayed only a few months. He wasn't remembered by any of the current crew, so once again Wyler sought out a supervisor. A humpbacked veteran of twenty years with the company and well past retirement age, Tomas Gunderson had seen them all come and go—the chairman of the board, account executives, and maintenance staff. To recall Beech he had to consult the time sheets. For Gunderson, the time sheets were as individual as fingerprints. From them he could not only identify Frank Beech but reconstruct his character and history.

"Beech. Sure. I remember now. A bad apple. Late. Always late. Did you a favor to come to work at all." Gunderson frowned as he shuffled the sheets. "Monday you could count him out automatically. When he did appear, he was sullen. Whenever you wanted him he was taking a smoke in the men's room. If you sent him upstairs to pick up a special, you didn't see him again for half an hour. Made a pest of himself with the secretaries. People are hard to get so we bend over backward not to fire anybody, but finally the word came down: Get rid of him."

"Why?" Wyler wanted to know. "What triggered it?"

Gunderson pursed his lips. He peered at the time sheets. The answer wasn't there.

Wyler tried the executive offices. Helene Parsons, executive secretary and in charge of office staff from receptionists to typists to private secretaries, was not available. She would be tied up in an executive conference till well into the afternoon, the pretty brunette at the reception desk told him.

"Can I help you?" She was all charm.

"I'm sure you can," he told her and showed her the open shield case. "I understand Stefanie Altman worked here about a year ago."

The receptionist waited warily.

"Did you know her?"

"Yes," she answered reluctantly and then hurried to qualify. "I knew her, of course, but not well. By that I mean we weren't friends particularly. We didn't see each other on the outside."

"Who were her friends? Whom did she see on the outside?"

"I don't know. I think you'd better talk to Ms. Parsons."

"Okay." He went over to one of the dark-green leather sofas and sat down.

The brunette's eyes opened wide. "You're going to sit here and wait?"

"If that's all right? It is all right, isn't it?"

Ms. Parsons emerged from her meeting at 2:00 P.M. promptly. She was blonde, sleek, carefully assembled; in her forties, but still smoldering, Wyler thought. She looked him over too and judged him worth a smile and routine charm. She waved for him to follow and once inside her private office indicated the chair beside her desk.

"I'm interested in anything you can tell me about Stefanie Altman," he began.

Parsons nodded, swiveled around to the filing cabinet on her right. The file she sought was readily and conveniently at hand. She placed it squarely and precisely in front of her and then opened it. "Ms. Altman came to us in June of '85 and stayed till September of '86. She resigned for personal reasons. She was quiet, reliable, a good worker." Ms. Parsons closed the file.

"That's all you can tell me?"

"She kept very much to herself."

"Do you think I waited over two hours for that?"

"How long you waited is not my fault nor concern."

His gray eyes bored into her, but she remained unperturbed.

"All right, then, what can you tell me about Frank Beech?"

A twitch, barely enough to crack the perfection of her maquillage, came and was quickly gone again.

"You are aware that on November thirtieth Stefanie Altman shot and killed an alleged mugger. That mugger was Frank Beech. The story was in all the papers and reported on television and the radio." Wyler was getting angry.

She sensed it. "Of course."

"Frank Beech was employed here. You must know that too. You must know that they both worked here at the same time. Surely, what you read and heard aroused your interest and caused you to refresh your memory about them. Actually, Ms. Parsons, I'm surprised that it didn't occur to anyone in this office to step forward with that information."

Helene Parsons flushed under her Number 2 Rachel powder base. "It was over a year ago. I don't believe anybody made the connection. Beech worked in the mail room."

"I've just come from the mail room," Wyler told her.

"According to Mr. Gunderson, Beech made a pest of himself with the secretaries up here. He got fired because of it."

"He annoyed the girls, yes. But as to why he got fired . . ."

"You had nothing to do with it?"

"With his getting fired? No. Of course not."

"Did Altman and Beech know each other?"

"If you're asking me about a personal relationship . . ."

"Come on, Ms. Parsons. You strike me as an extremely efficient lady. You are responsible for all the hiring and firing up here. You know what goes on."

"I don't pry into the personal lives of the employees."

She was lying, but why? "All right, Ms. Parsons. Right now the case against Stefanie Altman is very much in balance. It could go either way. She claims the man she killed was a stranger, but if, in fact, there was a previous connection between them, it could be very serious for her." Wyler gave Parsons a moment to respond; when she didn't, he got up and handed her his card. "When you decide it's your duty to help, call me."

Helene Parsons took the card, but her eyes were on Wyler and she flushed, deeply. "Frank Beech was slime. He deserved to die."

Quietly, Wyler sat down again.

"He chased everything in skirts—young or old, plain or pretty, married or single, with or without a boyfriend; he didn't give a damn, he went after her."

"He made a play for the women here in the office?"

"What do you think I'm talking about?" the executive secretary demanded.

"Did he make a play for you?"

She looked down.

"How about it, Ms. Parsons?" There was no way to make it easy for her even if he'd wanted to. "Did you and Beech have a sexual relationship?"

She nodded. Then raised her eyes. "I'm a widow. Five years ago I lost my husband. He had a heart attack—totally without warning. I was devastated. Lonely. You have no idea what being alone after years of a happy marriage can do to a woman." She shook her head as though to dispel the memories. "I was flattered by a young man's attention. He was handsome, you know, in a sleazy way, and he had plenty of sex appeal. God, it oozed out of him! So, I dated him a couple of times. That's all it took him to get me to bed. Oh, I resisted, but not that hard. I knew that it was either give in or lose him. At that point, I didn't want to lose him." She paused, swallowed, and said in a dry voice, "Hard to believe now." She even managed a thin smile. "It was rough sex from the very beginning. Then later it became degrading. But I put up with it. He was the one who . . . got bored. I could see the signs—he'd be late, or stand me up completely. He always made sure I'd find out he'd been with another woman. I could see the signs and I should have thrown him out. Instead, I let him dump me."

Wyler sympathized. There were men who got their kicks from humiliating women and women who allowed it, perhaps even needed to be subjugated like that. No use making Helene Parsons dwell on it.

"What about Stefanie Altman? Did she have a similar experience?"

And the tears welled up in Helene Parsons's eyes to thank him for moving on.

"It was worse for her. To start with, she was shy, very inhibited. Beech had trouble getting to her and that only aroused him more. She was a challenge, so he used different tactics. He pretended he was interested in improving himself. Showed himself as sensitive, eager to learn."

"Did you warn her? Obviously, you saw it happening."

"I didn't know her that well. She was a very private person. And I . . ." The secretary shook her head.

"Ms. Parsons," Wyler urged gently, "I can't believe you didn't warn her."

"All right. I tried. Actually, I found out the guys downstairs were making book on it! That was the last straw. I did talk to Stefanie. But it was too late. He'd foreseen it and given her his version first—which was that I had been the aggressor, that I'd come on to him. He told her he was the one who had broken off the relationship, which I couldn't deny, and that now I was jealous. Jealous of her, Stefanie Altman, for God's sake!"

"And then?"

"She believed him. The rest followed the pattern. Except . . ." Helene Parsons hesitated. "I think he may have been more than rough with her. Brutal. I think she must have been a virgin." Her whole body sagged. For a moment, the real woman behind the makeup was revealed.

"She didn't come in for nearly a week and then it was to quit. At that point I went to my boss and told him why she was leaving. He sent down word to get rid of Beech. I told Stefie. I tried to get her back, but she wouldn't change her mind. I told her she was safe, that Beech would never bother her again. But the associations were too strong, I suppose. Or maybe she'd found out about the bets."

Wyler understood that rape could never be an isolated incident. It was a violation that tainted every aspect of a woman's life and would haunt even the most rational, well-balanced woman. For someone as sensitive, idealistic, and sheltered as Stefanie Altman, it must have been devastating. To be raped on a bet, to be ridiculed, must have been beyond endurance. Yet Stefie Altman had borne it and recovered. Or so it seemed. She had quit the job at Williston and Coe, found the bookshop, made new friends, and met Timothy Kampel. She had guts, Wyler thought. Guts enough to avenge herself?

Wyler got up and held out his hand. "Thank you."

Helene Parsons took it. "I don't suppose this is the end?"

"I'm afraid not. The district attorney will want a formal deposition. Then if the case comes to trial . . ."

"I'll have to appear," she concluded. Then sighed once more. "This won't do Stefie any good, will it?"

*   *   *

Wyler headed directly to the squad. The lights were out in the lieut's office.

"Where is she?" he asked Art Potts.

"She left early to get ready for a big charity dinner at the Waldorf," Jacoby's aide told him. "Can it wait?"

"Sure. I suppose so." Wyler carefully hung up his camel hair overcoat, unwound the cashmere muffler, and placed his dark green fedora on the shelf above the rack. Then he sat down to type his report. He felt deflated.

CHAPTER
TWELVE

Norah Mulcahaney was seated on the dais along with, among others, the mayor, the police commissioner, the president of Hunter College, and Randall Tye, her escort. The president of Hunter College invited her to address the student body that Saturday. It was a heady evening. Too heady, Norah thought on awakening the next morning, temples throbbing and a dry, flannel taste in her mouth. After the dinner they'd gone on to the Oak Room at the Algonquin to hear Julie Wilson sing the old standards that brought back so many memories for Norah. She'd had champagne, not a lot but more than she was used to. And now she'd overslept for the second morning in a row. Norah swung her legs over the side of the bed and winced. Oh, God! It wasn't worth it.

She showered, drank black coffee, and skipped breakfast. She was dressed and on her way out when the phone rang. She hesitated. It was probably the squad. She was on her way, but . . . better to answer. By the time she reached the phone, it had stopped ringing. It made her feel even more guilty.

Again she managed to slip into the station house without being noticed. Except for the two new men, Nicolo Tedesco and Julius Ochs, the squad room was empty. They merely looked up and nodded as she passed through to her office. No one had missed her. She was both relieved and let down. Forget it, she told herself, and get to work.

First, she reviewed the chart. Then she picked up the Altman file.

Wyler's report both shocked and disappointed Norah. For all her cautioning him that they must be wary of taking sides, she couldn't help but see Altman as the victim and so want her cleared. But evidence of her previous knowledge of the man she had shot and killed was totally unexpected and devastating. It could convict Altman. John Douvas, the ADA assigned to the case, would ride the new evidence hard, Norah knew. She couldn't blame him. It was his job. But she continued to believe in the young woman. Yet Altman had lied, at least in part. Unless the new witness, Helene Parsons, was the one lying. Why would she do that? Why should she subject herself to the inevitable public embarrassment that acknowledgment of her relationship with Beech was bound to bring unless what she said was true? So, another interrogation of Stefanie Altman was called for. Wyler could bring her in. Norah checked her calendar: the grand jury hearing had been rescheduled for the coming Monday. Four days. Plenty of time. She turned to the Valente file.

Ferdi was making good progress, she thought as she read his report. He had located Imogene Davies's roommate and also identified the man in the photograph with Davies and Mrs. Valente. In her own investigation of Gilda Valente's society friends, Norah had not turned up even a hint of her interest and patronage of young artists, yet according to Mary Ruth Rae, it was no secret. In his personal memo to Norah, Arenas suggested the ex-country and gospel singer was more emotionally involved with her benefactress than she was willing to admit.

The phone rang.

"Lieutenant Mulcahaney? This is the office of the president of Hunter College calling. I'm Ivy Kessler. We'd like to confirm that you will be participating in the conference on Women and the Law this Saturday at one P.M.?"

"That's right."

"Your topic will be Women in Police Work. We have you down for a twenty-minute address to be followed by a question-and-answer period. Is that all right?"

"Yes, that's fine."

She wrote the title down at the head of a large, lined yellow pad. She settled herself to think about what she should say. Nothing came to her. At least, nothing she hadn't said before—over and over. Time passed. The pad remained unmarked. The phone rang again. This time she was glad of the interruption.

"It's Randall, Norah. How are you?"

"I've been better. Too much champagne."

"Come on. You had about three glasses."

"That's two more than I should have had," she replied ruefully.

"Okay, no more champagne for a while. Listen, I have tickets to the opening of the new musical from London, *A Tale of Two Cities.* How about it?"

"Not tonight, Randall, thanks. I've got work to catch up on. I need an early night."

"Okay. We'll forget the show and just have dinner. I'll get you home by nine. Promise."

"I don't know."

"I'll pick you up at your place at seven."

He was hard to resist, Norah thought. Charming, handsome, Randall Tye commanded attention everywhere they went. He'd started his career as a journalist working for a small New England daily. His ambition had been to own and publish his own newspaper, to be in a position to write what he thought, free of outside pressure. In essence, he wanted to exert influence. In the course of covering a presidential primary, Randall Tye appeared briefly on local television. The response came as a total surprise. There was something in his personality that communicated; there was empathy between him and the viewer. The calls and letters poured in. The impact of that one brief appearance was bigger than a byline or an editorial, and it was instantaneous. Randall Tye's goal shifted. He applied for

a job at that same local station and from then on his rise
was known to all.

Tye had carved a niche for himself in the television in-
dustry. Part journalist, he had covered politics and high
society, scandal, murder; he was at ease with heads of government, rock stars, athletes. Part editorialist, he did a
once-a-week, half-hour commentary on a subject of his
own choosing. Part performer, he appeared on others'
shows. In his current employment at the Liberty Network,
he combined them all.

At the beginning, when she'd started the series of PR
appearances, Norah Mulcahaney had felt out of her element. No longer. She was enjoying herself. She accepted
the applause, the admiring looks that followed her. Of
course, she was under no delusion. She knew it was all,
including Tye's attentions, predicated on the fact that she
was carrying the Valente case. The public deplored organized crime, yet was fascinated by the personalities of top
organized-crime figures. Once the case was cleared, the
spotlight would move on to somebody else. So why not
enjoy it while it lasted?

As long as the work didn't suffer. Nothing wrong with
enjoying herself as long as the work got done, she thought.
She opened the envelope Ferdi had left for her along with
his report. It contained copies of the photograph that had
been on Imogene Davies's desk. She placed the whole
thing in her handbag, taking care not to crease it.

Sitting around the office daydreaming was not getting
the work done.

As usual, Norah was met at the door of the Valente
penthouse by Salvatore Nunzio, who escorted her to the
study.

"What've you got for me, Lieutenant?" Dario Valente
asked as soon as his secretary had left and closed the door.

Without comment, Norah opened her handbag, selected one of the copies of his wife's picture and handed
it to him.

He studied it. "Who are these people?"

"You don't know?"

"No." Neither his expression nor his tone contradicted that.

"Perhaps Mrs. Sequi might be able to help."

He spoke into the intercom on his desk. "Ask Armanda to come in, please."

As before, Armanda Sequi appeared promptly. As before, she placed herself just inside the door, her eyes fixed on Valente, at his disposal.

He motioned her over. "Take a look at this picture. Do you know these people with Gilda?"

"No," she replied, first to Valente, then to Norah. "No, I don't."

"The woman was Mrs. Valente's hairdresser," Norah told them.

Valente questioned his aunt with a look, but she shook her head. "I certainly didn't know who did my wife's hair. I must say I'm surprised she had her picture taken with the woman. Maybe it was in the way of a testimonial, only then I would have expected her to autograph it."

"The woman in the picture, the hairdresser, is Imogene Davies. She jumped, fell, or was pushed from a window in her apartment Monday afternoon. It was in the papers."

Valente shook his head and spread his hands in a gesture disclaiming knowledge.

"No mention was made of her connection with Mrs. Valente," Norah explained. "But I'm sure it won't be long before it's known."

"Are you suggesting that the death of my wife and that of this . . . Imogene Davies . . . are linked in some way?"

"Ms. Davies called me Monday morning. She said she had information about Mrs. Valente. We made a date to meet at the Wollman Rink at one o'clock. She never appeared."

"Ah . . ." he sighed, still studying the picture. "Who's the man?"

"We have a name: Peter Hines. We know he was a

singer and a protégé of your wife, but we haven't located him yet."

"Ah, yes. One of the young music students she sponsored."

"You know about that?"

"Of course. Who do you think paid the bills?"

"I wish you'd told me."

"Why? These young people benefited from Gilda's interest. For one of them to kill her would have been to kill the goose that laid the golden eggs." He laughed, a short, derisive bark. "However, leave the picture."

Norah hesitated. Valente had a network of informants, of course. She personally couldn't hope to match it. To organize the resources of the department would take time.

"I can expedite your search, Lieutenant," Valente told her. "You aren't moving very fast, you know. In fact, you're not moving. It seems you have too many outside interests."

Norah flushed. Her chin came up aggressively. "That's not your business, Mr. Valente."

"It is if it's affecting the investigation into my wife's death."

"It isn't."

"I'm glad to hear it."

"Everything I'm doing is at the direct order of Chief Deland. All current investigations, including that of your wife's death, are covered; none of the work of the squad is being neglected."

"But surely it puts an added burden on you and on your people," he continued, somewhat more conciliatory. "Why not use the help I can offer? The truth is, we had a deal, Lieutenant." An edge crept into his manner. "But you're not delivering, and I'm getting impatient."

He was getting shortchanged; silently, Norah acknowledged it. She wasn't giving full concentration or maximum effort, not to this case and not to the Altman case either. She couldn't claim to be doing her best, because she wasn't. Also she shouldn't have come seeking this interview. She'd acted on impulse, without the proper preparation.

"Aside from this picture, do you have any other leads?" Valente wanted to know.

"No." She clenched her jaw. It was hard to admit. The case was ten days old and going nowhere.

"Then you need help," the *capo* concluded. "As a private citizen I have the right to ask questions, talk to anybody I want. That's what I'm going to do and what my people are going to do." He tapped the picture with his forefinger. "We're going to find this Peter Hines and find him fast." He forestalled Norah's protest.

"Of course, we'll turn him over to you."

Once again, she'd had no choice but to accept Valente's help, Norah thought as she left the Art Deco building, crossed the street, and entered the park. If he had been anyone else, no matter how important—a high government official, a top entertainer, a famous athlete—she could have stopped him. But Dario Valente's power derived from direct opposition to the law. She knew cooperation was expedient, but it made her uncomfortable. On the Tye show Norah had supported Valente's right to a full and vigorous investigation into his wife's death; working with him was something else. She didn't trust him. Oh, she believed he valued his word, but also that he was capable of specious reasoning, of twisting the facts to suit his needs.

Her path was only a few yards inside the park and ran parallel to the street, yet the traffic and noise seemed far away. The snow was nearly all gone. The air was redolent with the scent of damp earth, the breeze light and energizing. In spite of the big blizzard, Norah reminded herself, winter was officially still more than a week off. She slowed to a leisurely pace and thought back to her first meeting with Dario Valente. He had been in bed, exhausted by the long trek from his house in the country and the trauma of hearing of his wife's death. He hadn't mentioned she was pregnant. Later, he claimed he hadn't known and he'd explained, logically enough, that their hopes had already been raised and dashed twice, so Gilda had undoubtedly been trying to spare him yet another disappointment by not saying anything until she was absolutely sure. But he did know now, Norah reasoned. And he'd had plenty of time to think about it. He could have begun to wonder if in fact that was the reason Gilda had kept silent. Or if there was another, less innocent? Like his not being the father of the child. Could he have had doubts about his wife's fidelity even before Norah told him she was pregnant?

Either way, she shouldn't have shown him the photograph. It had been a mistake.

What could she do about it?

She called Ferdi Arenas.

"We've got to locate Peter Hines, fast. I want every available man on this. Let's see." She took a look at the assignments and transferred five detectives. "Start with the top agents in concert and opera. Ask them about Peter Hines. It's a small, closed world; everybody knows everybody else. Send a couple of men to the Met and the State Theater at Lincoln Center. Let them ask around. We just want to know where we can find him. Don't mention the Valente case or Imogene Davies. No pressure. But move."

"Right, Lieutenant."

The sinking sensation she'd felt at the pit of her stomach since talking to Valente persisted.

"When you find him, let me know. Right away."

"Where will you be?"

The question, innocent enough, stung her. She had a taping scheduled and then she had the dinner with Randall. Should she cancel? The dinner at least?

"I'll leave a number," she said.

Going on patrol, it was called when the whip or squad commander went to his favorite watering hole, Ferdi thought. This was not the same, of course not, he knew it, he knew Norah Mulcahaney, but the others . . . He tried to hide his anxiety and—yes, his disappointment.

Norah sensed disapproval and it hurt. She had taken

it for granted that it was known she was doing PR work by order of the chief. It hadn't occurred to her that it would look as if she had been seduced by the glamour and fame. She flushed and started to explain, then stopped. She wasn't required to justify herself, certainly not to Ferdi. She shouldn't have to—not to him. "Is that all right with you, Sergeant?"

"Whatever you say, Lieutenant." A nerve at the corner of his mouth twitched.

She had set up the operation, made the assignments; it was his job to carry it through. "You have a problem with any of this?"

"No problem, Lieutenant."

The frown still etched deep, Norah sent for Simon Wyler.

"What's Stefanie Altman's reaction to the Parsons statement?"

"I haven't talked to her about it, Lieutenant. I thought you'd want to handle that yourself."

"Yes, right." It would be best, Norah thought. It was her responsibility to conduct that interrogation. At least no one had challenged Altman's assertion that Beech and his buddies had accosted her. *They* had approached *her*. Stefanie could hardly have anticipated the encounter.

"How about the knife?" Norah asked.

Wyler shook his head. "No trace."

"That leaves the ski mask," Norah mused aloud. "It was off and lying beside the body when the RMPs arrived. Altman claims she pulled it off in her attempt to give Beech mouth to mouth. We need to know if he was in fact wearing it when he approached her. Pesrow won't say. Maybe the man who was with them will." She took a long, deep breath and exhaled slowly. "If we ever find him. Any leads?"

"No, Lieutenant. I went over to Acme, but nobody remembers Beech or Pesrow or anybody hanging around for any length of time."

"You checked the employment applications?"

"Yes, Lieutenant. There were forty-nine that morning.

Thirty of them were sent out on calls. Of the nineteen left, Pesrow and Beech were two. I'm still running down the seventeen."

"Good." Norah thought it over. She couldn't afford to put extra men on a case that was all but closed. "Stay with it."

Wyler was disappointed. He had expected that she would give him help, but he left without saying anything.

Shortly after, Norah left too. For the first time she could remember, for the first time ever, Norah Mulcahaney was glad to close her office door and walk away.

The taping took place nearby at the ABC-TV studios on Sixty-seventh Street and was quickly done. She had plenty of time to go back to the squad, but she went home instead.

The days in the spotlight had taught Norah a lot about the kind of appearance she was expected to present. She had learned makeup for both on and off camera, day and night, for official appearances and private, intimate dinners. In a week she had bought more clothes than she had in a couple of years. And what clothes! The clothes she bought for work—after all, you never knew when the camera would be on you—were her usual pants suits, but better tailored and more expensive. It was the night dressing that was exciting. She was buying and wearing the kind of outfits she'd never even dreamed about. She entered shops that had previously awed her. She spent sums that seemed outrageous; her new life style had not changed her values. Actually, she was offered outfits free simply for the publicity the designer and the store would get by her wearing them. But Norah knew better. She paid for what she wore, including a sumptuous, long-haired, pale beige coyote coat.

Dressed for her evening with Randall Tye, Norah looked herself over in the long glass on the back of the bedroom door. She was wearing the latest of her acquisitions—a cream-colored, long-sleeved, low-bosomed satin gown. Her dark hair was loose on her shoulders; a new tint of blue eye shadow intensified the blue of her eyes;

the gentle shading of dark powder softened the jaw line. She liked what she saw. At the same time it made her uneasy.

That night Randall took her to the opening of yet another waterside restaurant. They were greeted with the usual adulation and obsequious courtesy, seated at the most desirable window table. The ambience was warm and charming, the view of lower Manhattan spectacular.

The wine was served. Randall raised his glass. They drank. He was utterly handsome, charming, she thought, a real celebrity. He could go anywhere, was welcomed in the finest restaurants, the trendiest discos, the most elegant of private parties. He could get fifth-row center seats for the biggest Broadway hit at a moment's notice. He was the perfect escort—attentive, solicitous. He didn't table hop. He didn't participate in conversations in which she couldn't take part. When they were together he did not allow himself to be distracted from her. In sum, he was the perfect escort. So why wasn't she having a good time?

The fault lay with her, not with him. He was in another league. No matter that she was dressed up in satin and fur, she didn't belong in it. No matter how many fancy parties he took her to, how often her name appeared in the gossip columns, she never would. She wasn't sure she wanted to.

"Norah?"

She had been looking out over the dark water to the skyline of lower Manhattan without seeing its spectacular beauty. Now, she blinked and turned. "Did you say something?"

"Several things. You're a million miles away, Norah."

"Sorry. Actually, I shouldn't be here. I should be working. Will you excuse me, Randall?"

"You mean you want to leave?"

"Yes. Forgive me. I have to get back. I have to get back and help Ferdi with the canvassing at Lincoln Center. I have to get back and talk to Stefanie Altman." Suddenly, she couldn't wait.

"We just arrived."

"I know. I apologize. Honestly, I can't stay." She started to get up, reaching for the coat draped over the back of her chair. "You stay. Please, I insist."

"You can't just walk out like this." Tye looked around. "What will people say?"

She was surprised. "I don't care. I didn't think you would either."

"I don't." His eyes swept the other diners. "Not about them. But there are certain considerations. We're guests here, Norah, invited guests. We can't just walk out."

"You mean our dinner is on the house?"

"What's wrong with that?"

Norah stared at him.

"It comes with the job."

"Not with my job."

"Come on, Norah, you've been on this PR kick long enough to know what gives. You're enjoying it. Don't tell me you aren't."

"No, I can't tell you that. But it's over." All at once, she was sure of herself. "All over. I'm through with it." She was putting the coat on.

Tye looked nervously toward the entrance door where he saw the maitre d' watching. "I don't know what's come over you."

"I've got work to do, that's all. I've been neglecting it. I'm not going to neglect it anymore."

"All right. Fine. We'll have our dinner, then I'll take you back to your office, or home, or whatever you want. Just don't storm out like this."

"There's no reason why you can't stay, if it matters so much to you."

"I don't want everybody to know we had a fight."

"Is that what this is?"

He sighed lugubriously. "All right, you win. We'll leave now." He raised a hand to summon the captain. "Will you have my car brought around, please. Lieutenant Mulcahaney has received an urgent call from her office."

They were bowed out with the same deference with

which they had been ushered in. It seemed to satisfy Randall Tye.

"Where to, Lieutenant?" he asked as he handed her into the chauffeured limousine.

She couldn't go back to the squad in these clothes, Norah thought. She'd have to change. "Home, please."

Randall gave the address, then sat back against the luxurious upholstery. He said not another word till, as they emerged from the tunnel on the Manhattan side, the car phone rang.

"For you," he said, and handed it to Norah.

It was Arenas. As she listened, the color drained from her face.

CHAPTER THIRTEEN

Norah gripped the phone hard to keep her hand from shaking.

Beside her in the limousine as it continued smoothly up the East River Drive, Randall Tye lit a cigarette and looked out the window, trying to dissociate himself from her conversation. He couldn't, of course, but she appreciated the attempt. He must know the call was urgent and was likely to concern a homicide. She needed to get to the scene as quickly as possible, but if she asked him to take her there, would he agree not to use information so conveniently dropped into his lap? That Randall accepted favors as a matter of course disturbed Norah. His attitude tonight had surprised and disappointed her. It was a side of him she had not suspected. Nevertheless, she was sure of one thing about Randall Tye: He was a dedicated newsman, as professional about his job as she was about hers. He would not abuse their personal relationship.

"Make the usual notifications," she told Ferdi Arenas. "I'm on my way." She hung up. "Randall, I need to go to Ninety-ninth between Madison and Park."

Without comment, Tye relayed the change to the chauffeur. When they reached the corner of Ninety-ninth, he could hardly fail to notice the crowd on the street and the parked RMPs, nor fail to identify the lineup of cars at the curb as official. Yet when they pulled up and he handed her out, all he said was:

"Good luck."

Their eyes met. His eyes told her to trust him. She nodded and watched while he got back into the car and the chauffeur closed the door. Then she turned her back on Randall Tye.

Norah Mulcahaney in her luxurious fur coat surveyed the area. The neighborhood was typically New York— part high-rise, luxury condos and part tenements. It had started, she assumed, as affluent and degenerated into near slum. With living space so scarce, gentrification had spread to it. However, the narrow, five-story red brick building in which the crime had been committed had not yet been affected. It slumped wearily between more fortunate edifices. Its façade was grimy, the bars on the downstairs windows rusted, the glass behind them cracked. *Parkside.* The lettering, once grand in gold leaf, was all but illegible. Norah judged the crowd bundled against the cold to be from the tenements; not that the rich people weren't curious, just that they would be watching from inside.

She crossed the street and approached the uniform at the front door. In her small, beaded evening purse, Norah carried her shield case and her off-duty gun, a .22, small but powerful at short range.

"Where is it?" she asked.

"Ah . . ." He stared first at the gold shield then at her. "Ground floor rear, Lieutenant."

His response reminded Norah of how she was dressed. She got a few more startled looks as she passed inside, but nobody commented. Certainly, nobody dared whistle, not after Arenas spotted her and called out.

"This way, Lieutenant."

The place was a shambles, furniture overturned, pictures askew, glass shattered. It could have been a fight or wanton destruction, Norah thought as she picked her way over to where the victim lay. He was sprawled on the floor, upper body resting against the base of the sofa, apparently as he had fallen, reeling from the final, vicious blow. His face was a battered, bloody pulp discolored from the dark brown of dried blood to the purple of subcutaneous hemorrhaging. Yet she recognized him as the man in the photograph with Imogene Davies and Gilda Valente. Peter Hines had been outstandingly good-looking. Norah shivered and drew her coat around her. He wasn't good-looking anymore.

Henry Yost, assistant medical examiner, closed his bag and struggled to his feet. Yost winced, but whether out of pity for the victim or from the pain of his arthritic knees, Norah couldn't tell. Everybody knew Yost was having trouble getting around, but he refused to be restricted to the lab. He insisted on taking his turn in the field, and Norah waited till he had himself in hand.

"Could one person have done all this damage?" she asked.

"I'd say two were involved. Both pros."

Another chill passed through Norah. She stuffed her hands into the coat pockets. Valente's pros? But pros didn't exert themselves, didn't work this hard if the intent was to kill. "A bullet or a knife would have been less trouble, don't you think?"

"Maybe they got carried away." Yost shrugged.

She sighed. "At least we won't have any trouble fixing the time." She looked to Ferdi. "The whole building must have heard the commotion."

"I haven't had a chance to talk to the neighbors."

"Who called in the complaint?"

"Nobody." Ferdi threw out his hands in frustration. "I traced him through the City Center Opera Company. He'd auditioned for them back in September. I came over. Rang. Got no answer. I came up and found the door unlocked. I walked in. It was . . ." He consulted his notebook. " . . . eight-twenty P.M."

"Nobody called in," Norah repeated thoughtfully. "But somebody must have heard. This wasn't just one loud bang. This lasted awhile. Maybe the neighbors didn't know what was going on; maybe they didn't want to know, but for sure somebody heard." She took a deep breath. "Okay, call in Tedesco and Ochs and the rest of them. I want this building canvassed from top to bottom and the buildings on either side, too. Don't miss anybody."

"Can you give me a time of death?" she asked Yost.

He hesitated. "I'd rather not, not without further examination. It's very cold in here, in case you hadn't noticed."

She certainly had. What she noticed now was that the window was open and, touching the radiator, she found that it was stone cold. Yet she heard a loud clanking in the pipes that suggested there was steam somewhere in the system. Norah's attention had been on the victim and on the destruction around him; now she looked at the apartment. It consisted of three rooms, small, badly in need of painting and plastering. The furniture was cheap, scratched and gouged; the studio couch sagged. No piano, not even an upright. Hines might once have been a protégé of Gilda Valente's, but no more.

"Is it possible he fought back?" she asked Yost.

"If you're thinking of skin under the fingernails or traces of the perp's blood or hair, or anything like that, I believe we can rule it out. He was overmatched. The instinct would have been to huddle in on himself and ward off the blows rather than try to retaliate. In fact"—the assistant ME pointed—"the blows came down on him so hard, they broke the fingers of one hand."

Her instinct was to turn away from the bloody, crushed hand, but she forced herself to take a good look. To fix the image. Then she told the forensics detectives, "I want every piece of broken furniture dusted and the upholstery vacuumed."

Long after the body of Peter Hines was removed, the search for microscopic evidence went on. Long after the forensic team had packed up their equipment and left, the interrogation of the tenants continued. The halls were dark; if the odor was an indication of what the darkness hid, it was just as well. Inside the apartments, most tenants were making an effort to keep ahead of rot and decay, but it was clear that some were giving up. In buildings like this, people were mistrustful of the police, resistant to questioning. But tonight, when they opened the door to find a woman in an elegant fur coat and long satin gown on the doorstep, they didn't know what to make of it. Norah gritted her teeth and persevered; she promised herself she would never be caught like this again.

Meantime, the job had to be done. By her straightforward manner and diligent questioning, not overlooking Ferdi Arenas's official gravity in backing her up, she convinced the witnesses that she was not playing a game. But she didn't get many answers.

Four statements were finally elicited. Four tenants admitted to having been home and hearing the commotion: two housewives and two working men—a department store security guard and a construction worker. They agreed the noise had started at about 6:00 P.M.; the women fixing the time because they were just about to put supper on the table and the men because they'd turned on the six o'clock news. They all agreed it was over quickly. Within minutes. The security guard volunteered that one of the apartments was being renovated and he thought that was the reason for the banging.

"Renovated?" Ferdi was openly disbelieving. "Who're you kidding? You weren't born the last time any renovation was done around here."

The construction worker offered the same excuse for ignoring the commotion.

"The only way to renovate this place would be to tear it down and start over," Ferdi said. "You should know that."

Norah merely raised her eyebrows.

One of the housewives, a young mother, Maria Hernandez, did admit the noise woke up her baby and started him crying. At that point she did wonder what the sounds might indicate. But before she could do anything, the noise stopped.

In sum, nobody knew anything. Nobody so much as put an eye to the peephole of a door, much less opened the door to look out, because nobody wanted to know anything. It was that kind of building. It was the kind of building and the kind of neighborhood where loud noises, even screams, weren't unusual. A bang in the street wasn't likely to be a backfire and people knew it and learned not to be curious, to keep their eyes and ears closed, but above all to keep their mouths shut. At any rate, the quasiwitnesses agreed that the noise, whatever it was, was over in five minutes at the most. Naturally they were relieved. Until this moment, they'd forgotten all about it.

At 1:00 A.M. Norah called off the canvass and asked Ferdi to drive her home. For a while they drove in companionable silence, then as she had done so many times before, Norah began to sort out her thoughts aloud.

"About this Mary Ruth Rae: if she lived with Davies, and Hines was both Davies's old boyfriend and a protégé of Gilda Valente's, it's hard to believe she didn't know where he lived."

Ferdi nodded. "Oh, she knew all right. She also knew we wouldn't have that much trouble finding him. I figure she was buying time. But for what . . ."

They both saw it at the same moment—a silver stretch limousine parked in front of Norah's door.

"Pull up behind," she told Ferdi.

As he did so, the rear door of the limo opened and a man came over.

"What are you doing here?" she demanded, trying to hold back her anger.

"Waiting for you," Randall Tye said, and smiled ingratiatingly.

She stared at him long and hard before speaking again. "It's late and I'm tired." She got out. "We'll talk another time."

Ferdi had come around and now stood at Norah's shoulder.

Tye ignored him. "Have you eaten?" he asked Norah.

"No."

"I figured you wouldn't have, so I brought supper." At

his nod, the chauffeur emerged and handed Tye a flat cardboard container.

"I'm not hungry.

"You can always find room for pizza." He waited. "This is not on the cuff," he assured her. "I paid for it myself."

She had to smile.

He seized on it. "I'll come up. I'll stay as long as it takes to make some coffee and warm this—it's stone cold by now—then I'm gone." Suddenly he acknowledged Ferdi's presence. "You're welcome to join us, Sergeant. There's plenty for all."

Arenas looked to Norah.

"It's okay, Ferdi. I'll see you in the morning, first thing."

Ferdi went around to his car and got in, but he waited till Norah had unlocked her front door and Randall Tye, carrying the pizza, followed her inside. He waited while the chauffeur returned to the limo, slid down in the driver's seat, and closed his eyes for a nap. Reassured, he turned on the ignition and headed for home.

Upstairs, Norah turned on the lights. She took off her fur coat and hung it, along with Tye's London Fog, in the hall closet. She kicked off her high heels and replaced them with well-worn, very comfortable slippers. Then she led the way to the kitchen, motioned to Tye to put the pizza down on the table but didn't light the oven.

"I really don't want to eat and I don't think you do either."

"No," Randall Tye admitted. "I'm here because I'm sorry for what happened tonight. If I seemed to be ridiculing your standards, I didn't mean to. In fact, I admire your integrity. I admire you, Norah Mulcahaney. I never met anybody like you."

"Well . . . thank you."

"The people I meet, most of them, are out for everything they can get. They figure it was a hard road up and when they finally make it to the top—hell, they're entitled!

They don't see anything wrong with accepting a free meal, free tickets, free trips. Most of the people I run with don't work hard at their jobs. Maybe they did at one time, but no more. They're riding on the past. It's not like that with you. Your road is still unfolding ahead. You've come a long way, but you're going a lot farther."

"That's very nice, Randall, thank you, but it remains to be seen."

"I saw all I needed tonight. The way you dropped everything. The way you ran to the scene. I was impressed."

"It shouldn't have happened. I shouldn't have had to go dressed like this."

"What difference does it make how you were dressed?"

"It was unsuitable. It showed a lack of sensitivity. I've got two big cases; I should have been at the squad or at home. Not out *dining.*"

"You were available."

"You don't understand. Never mind."

"I do understand, better than you think, but I don't agree. You're being too hard on yourself. You're entitled to a life outside the job."

"Not if it's in conflict."

"It doesn't have to be. Listen to me, Norah, darling. I know what you're going through. I know because I've been there. We're more alike than you realize." He paused. His clear amber eyes fixed on her. "We'd make a great team."

"Team?"

"I've fallen for you, Norah. Hard."

She caught her breath. She couldn't deny that she'd been thrilled by Randall Tye's attention. She'd even allowed herself to daydream about him, but not for long. She'd reminded herself that for Tye she was just another guest on his show, a short-term celebrity, and his courtesy was part of his job. Had she been wrong? Her heart beat fast.

"I don't know what to say, Randall. I don't go in for casual affairs."

"Believe me, my interest is far from casual."

"It's a question of how you define casual."

"I understand. I do," he hastened to assure her. "You can't be too careful nowadays. I promise you I don't indulge in promiscuous sex. I never have. Also, I've been tested and I'm clean."

Norah felt a hot flush of embarrassment. "I didn't mean . . . I wasn't thinking of that."

"What then?"

"You cited my ethics. Morality goes along with them. I don't believe in sex outside marriage."

His mouth actually fell open. "Come on, you don't mean it."

"I do."

"Your husband died . . . how long ago?"

"Four years."

He swallowed. Licked his lips and swallowed again. "So, let's get married."

It was Norah's turn to gape. "You don't mean that."

"Sure, I do. Why not?"

"For one thing, you're a glamorous television personality. I'm a working cop."

"Listen, don't let the glamour part fool you. I'm a working stiff just like you. Or I used to be. What you and the public see is the ten percent off the top; underneath it's digging, interviewing, researching. I chase down a story like you do a case. Our jobs are more alike than you know."

"And the hours?"

"Equally unpredictable."

"How about conflict of interest?"

"Shouldn't arise. I don't intend to divulge privileged information and I won't expect you to tip me off to an impending bust. What do you say, Norah? Shall we do it?"

"We've known each other less than two weeks."

"I know you better than some women I've dated for two years—and I haven't been celibate."

"But I don't know you. That is, I know you in your environment. I need to know you within mine."

"Then let's get started."

He reached across the table, got up, drew her around to him. Norah didn't resist. He kissed her and she returned the kiss tentatively, perhaps even shyly, almost with curiosity. As he grew more demanding, she broke off.

"Are you afraid of sex?" Randall Tye asked.

Norah flushed. "Maybe. Yes. It's been a long time."

"Don't worry about it. It's the kind of thing you don't forget. Believe me."

"Maybe, but not tonight. I'm sorry, Randall. I'm not ready for this."

Immediately, he let her go. "Whatever you say, sweetheart. But think about it. I said before you've come a long way in your career, but you can go a lot farther. I could help you. You have no idea how much a name dropped casually on radio or TV can count for. How people notice and remember. I know all about rabbis in the police department. I take it you have one."

A rabbi was someone higher up, one of the brass, who looked out for you and helped you get the good assignments, a patron, in other words. In Norah's case it was Inspector James Felix. She couldn't deny that over the years, Jim Felix had been her rabbi as he had been Joe's before. It was a generally accepted practice. There was nothing to be ashamed of, yet she didn't like the way Randall had presented it.

"I'll be your rabbi in the news media. You'll be amazed at what friendly attention from the media can do for you."

"I'm already amazed at what it's done to me," she said.

Not grasping her meaning, he brushed it aside. "We'll make a great team."

Norah grinned. "Is this a marriage proposal or are we negotiating a business deal?"

"Both. Smart girl. Both, and that's why it's going to work."

"No." Norah shook her head. "It's not."

"Shh . . ." He put his hand gently over her mouth. "Not another word. You're tired. You've got a new case. No, no," he hurried on. "I don't know anything about it and

I don't want you to tell me. Not now. One more quick kiss and I'm gone."

This was a mere, fleeting brush of the lips. Norah waited till the door closed softly and firmly behind him. She sighed.

The mating game. Manhattan style.

She started to laugh softly, and laughing, she padded into the bedroom, undressed, and slid wearily into bed.

CHAPTER
FOURTEEN

Tired as she was, Norah slept fitfully. Tye's proposal hovered at the edge of her subconscious. Apparently, it had affected her more than she realized. It shouldn't, she thought on awakening; Tye had been in and out of three marriages that she knew of. For him it was a transient state, a convenience for sex. Just the same, she lay in bed in the gray light before sunrise and allowed herself to imagine what marriage to Randall Tye might be like. But it could never be anything but fantasy, she thought, and threw back the covers to the coldness of the room and the real world.

She put on the radio to the news and kept it on while she showered and fixed breakfast but heard nothing about Peter Hines. Evidently, the media regarded it as one more instance of routine violence, not worth special attention. Sooner or later, however, the connection to Gilda Valente would be made and then there would be plenty of commotion, a demand for information. Would Randall take part in it?

Just what was Peter Hines's connection with Gilda?

Norah sat down to her usual breakfast of cereal, tiger's milk, a banana, and coffee; easy to fix and with plenty of staying power. Afterward, she dressed, choosing a pants suit out of her old wardrobe—a heathery tweed wool, warm and comfortable. She arrived at the squad at seven-thirty-five and went directly to her office. At eight she intended to call Jim Felix.

She'd planned what she would say to him. All she needed to do was jot down a couple of points she wanted to be sure not to forget. Then, while she waited, she got out the Valente file once again and stared at the photograph of the three happy young people. All three of them smiling, all three of them dead.

Once it was known that Gilda Valente was pregnant but hadn't told her husband, the possibility that she'd had a lover was just about automatic. But everyone testified to Gilda's love for and loyalty to her husband. There was no hint of suspicion attached to her movements, except for those infrequent absences from the meetings of her various committees, and they were so scattered, so irregular, that Norah had dismissed them. With the brutal beating and murder of Peter Hines, she must reexamine everything. Hines was linked to Gilda by way of the photograph and the testimony of Mary Ruth Rae. The gangland-style beating that resulted in his death pointed to Gilda's husband and completed the circle.

Assume that Hines had had an affair with Gilda. Assume he was the father of her child. If he'd wanted out, he wouldn't have had to kill her; all he would have had to do was deny the child was his. Gilda would hardly have been likely to demand he admit it. On the contrary, she would have been terrified to have her husband find out, and that would have put Hines in a perfect position to blackmail her. But his life style certainly didn't point to a hidden source of income. If anything, Norah thought, it should have happened the other way—Gilda should have killed Hines.

Norah went back out to the coffee machine, got herself a cup, and brought it back. Though she'd occupied the cubicle that was her office for a year and a half, she still relished the privacy and relative quiet. At this moment, before the start of the eight-to-four shift, she could actually hear the ticking of the big wall clock at the far end of the squad room. She tried the coffee, then set it aside because it was too hot.

If Valente had known his wife was pregnant by another man, he would have found that man and flayed him alive, cut his flesh up into pieces and dumped it along with the filth and refuse that his scows carried out to sea each day and unloaded into the deep waters past the Ambrose Light. Then, afterward, he would have killed her.

Dario Valente claimed to be dedicated to finding his wife's murderer, to avenging her. He had, however, agreed to take no direct action himself but to cooperate with the police. Being who he was, shouldn't he have demanded somebody higher up to take charge of the investigation? Somebody who, if not with more experience, at least had more clout than Norah? Had Valente accepted Norah so readily for the very reason that he didn't think much of her? That he could use her? Maybe he suspected his wife's infidelity? So why not let the police find his wife's lover, if she had one? And who would be more useful to this purpose, more sympathetic and gullible, distracted by her own celebrity, than Lieutenant Norah Mulcahaney?

And hadn't she in fact fingered Hines for the Mafia boss?

If she hadn't shown Valente the photograph, would Hines still be alive?

She no longer heard the ticking of the clock outside; the voices of the detectives coming to work sounded far away. Norah forgot about her eight o'clock call to Jim Felix and the speech she'd rehearsed for him. The way she saw it, whatever the relationship between Hines and Gilda Valente, he was innocent of her death. So if Valente had ordered the beating, he had not only punished the wrong man, he had broken his word to Norah. Therefore, she was no longer bound by their "deal." She need feel no obligation to a man whose power derived from evil. She felt, suddenly, free.

She sat up straight, squared her shoulders, and raised her chin.

Where was Ferdi? She'd told him she'd see him first thing this morning. What was holding him up?

The phone rang as though in direct response.

"It's Ferdi, Lieutenant. I had to take Concepción to the hospital. She's in labor. I have to stay."

"Of course you do. Give Concepción my love and call me as soon as the baby arrives."

"Thanks, Norah."

She felt a sharp, bittersweet pang, a mix of happiness for Ferdi and his wife tinged with the regret that she would never have a child herself. But she had made her peace with that. She reached for the coffee container and drank the contents in one long draught, never noticing it had gone cold. Then she settled for a thorough review of Ferdi's reports and his notes.

Norah entered the marbled vestibule and rang the bell marked RAE.

"Who is it?"

"Police, Ms. Rae. Lieutenant Mulcahaney. May I come up?"

The hesitation was slight, but the response carried more than a hint of annoyance. "I suppose so."

The buzzer, however, sounded promptly to release the lock. Norah located the red and gold elevator and rode up. Mary Ruth Rae was waiting in the open doorway. She was wearing well-tailored black wool slacks and a white silk shirt. The sun streaming through tall windows behind her silhouetted her voluptuous figure, and the backlighting provided her tangled red curls with an orange aura. No dark roots, Norah thought.

"I don't mean to be ungracious, Lieutenant . . . uh?"

"Mulcahaney."

"Yes. I haven't much time; I'm expecting my voice coach." She let Norah into the tiny foyer but no farther.

"I'll be as brief as I can," Norah promised, and strode purposefully past the singer and into the long, narrow, bright salon. She looked around with interest. She noted, as Ferdi had, the concert grand, the expensive carpets, the understated elegance, and contrasted it with Peter Hines's miserable apartment. She could imagine Gilda Valente, exquisitely groomed, with her furs and jewels, in this ambience, but never in that other place. She couldn't even imagine Gilda getting out of a taxi and crossing the pavement to his front door. Yet according to the report, both singers had been her protégés and benefited from her largesse. However, with Gilda gone, it appeared Mary Ruth Rae was about to change her life style.

"Moving?" Norah indicated the cartons stacked in a corner, the sheet music piled on the coffee table, the light rectangles on the walls where pictures had hung.

The redhead flushed and the freckles became visible through the makeup. "I'm just getting rid of . . ." She sighed. "What's the use? I might as well tell you. The apartment's paid for till next May. But the only way I can afford to go on living here and to continue with my lessons is to sell some of this stuff."

"It belongs to you?"

"She gave it to me." Mary Ruth tossed her head. "Mrs. Valente did. Gilda. I wouldn't be selling it if it wasn't mine. Honestly." Anxiety crept into her brown eyes. "You don't think he's going to want it back? Mr. Valente, I mean?"

"I couldn't say."

"It is mine. She gave it to me. What should I do? Should I offer to turn everything over to him?"

"I can't advise you."

Mary Ruth frowned. "I don't think Mr. Valente even knew about this place."

Norah had been on the verge of asking just that.

"I suppose he knew his wife sponsored young artists, helped them get started in their careers," the singer explained. "She was a patron of the arts in the classic sense. Know what I mean?"

"I'm not sure."

"The way kings and princes did in olden times."

Just for the satisfaction of nurturing talent? Norah wondered. It was a way of establishing a position both in society and the arts. "This is an elegant layout. Did Mrs. Valente set up all her protégés like this?"

"This wasn't exclusively for me, Lieutenant!" the redhead was quick to disclaim. "This apartment was . . . well, I lived here, yes, but Gilda, Mrs. Valente, used it as an office. For private business."

"What kind of private business?"

"Meetings and so forth. I don't know. Private."

"Business she couldn't transact at home?"

"I didn't ask questions. It was her apartment. She paid the rent. She could do whatever she wanted."

"You didn't care?"

Mary Ruth Rae looked earnestly at Norah. "You have to understand what knowing Mrs. Valente meant to me. I come from a little town you never heard of—Claymore, West Virginia. It's coal country, or was; it's all worked out now. My people are dirt farmers. I used to sing in church. I tried gospel singing, then country-western, but nobody thought that much about my voice, me least of all. I came to New York to get away from the farm. I never expected to make real money singing, but I didn't know how to do anything else. I got a few gigs in cheap nightclubs in Newark and Bayonne, places like that. Then I moved in with Imogene and she introduced me to Mrs. Valente. She heard me. Got all excited. Hired me a coach, set up auditions, got me started. I'm not ready for the Met, I know that, but without her I would never even have dreamed of trying."

"So Imogene Davies knew Mrs. Valente first."

"That's right."

"Do you know Dario Valente? Have you ever met him?"

"No."

"Do you know any of Mrs. Valente's other protégés?"

"Peter, of course, Peter Hines. I told the other detective, Sergeant Arenas, about him."

"Hines also met Mrs. Valente through Imogene Davies?"

"Yes."

"You told Sergeant Arenas that Ms. Davies was very jealous, that she thought you'd stolen her boyfriend."

"I also told him it wasn't true. There's nothing between Peter and me. Never was."

"How about between Hines and Mrs. Valente?"

"You'll have to ask Peter."

"Was Peter Hines one of those with whom Gilda Valente had business in this apartment?"

The singer flushed. "I've already answered that. I don't know what Gilda did or didn't do when she was alone here." She looked at her watch. "My voice coach is due any minute. Why don't you talk to Peter?"

"I'm afraid that's not possible. Peter Hines is dead."

Mary Ruth Rae went completely still. The color drained from her face. She stood like that for several moments. "What happened? Was it an accident?"

"He was severely beaten."

"Oh, my God." Mary Ruth closed her eyes and swayed. Norah put out a hand to steady her and at the touch she opened her eyes and allowed herself to be led to and helped into a chair.

"He was killed?"

"We believe he died as a result of his injuries."

She seemed still to find it hard to believe. "When? When did it happen?"

"Last night. Early. Some time after six."

"But I talked to him yesterday. Yesterday afternoon." She said it as though that made his dying a few hours later impossible. "Sergeant Arenas had asked me about Imogene. Peter's name came up. So I called him."

"To warn him? To get your stories together?"

"No, nothing like that."

"You also told Sergeant Arenas you didn't know where to reach Peter Hines."

She sighed heavily. "I know. I'm sorry. I was upset. I needed time to think."

"About what, Ms. Rae? You needed time to think about what? Peter's relationship with Gilda Valente? The use to which this apartment was put? Your relationship with Mrs. Valente?"

But Mary Ruth Rae had something else on her mind. "If I had given the sergeant Peter's address, would he . . . would that have made a difference?"

Norah couldn't answer; only a short while ago she had asked herself a similar question.

"What did you do after you called Hines?"

"I went to aerobics class, then had a sandwich and went to *Le Nozze di Figaro.* I'm studying the role of . . ."

"You were alone?"

"Yes." Her eyes widened. "You don't think . . . you can't think . . ."

"That you killed Peter Hines? No, Ms. Rae. You seem strong and fit, but I doubt you could have inflicted the injuries that Peter Hines sustained. But if you're holding anything back, I have to advise you that it's not a good idea."

"I'm not holding anything back."

"Good. Where were you on the night of November thirtieth?"

She didn't need to be told what made that night memorable. "That was a terrible night. Nobody would go out on a night like that unless they absolutely had to."

"Did anyone call you?"

"No." Mary Ruth Rae sighed.

"How about the next Monday, the seventh, in the afternoon? That was a very beautiful day. Everyone who could get out was out. Where were you between one and three P.M.?"

"That's when Imogene jumped, isn't it? And you're asking me for an alibi. I don't have an alibi. Does this mean you think she didn't jump? Who would want to kill Imogene? Why?"

"You can't think of a reason?"

The singer hesitated. "No," she said finally, "because I don't think anyone pushed her. I think she took her own life. And I'm sorry, Lieutenant, but I have no more time."

She turned and began to sort through a pile of sheet music on the piano bench.

"I would like you to make up a list of all the people who had business with Mrs. Valente in this apartment," Norah told her.

Mary Ruth Rae stopped what she was doing, but didn't turn around. "I can't remember. I didn't see them all. I wasn't here a lot of the time." The music sheet she held crackled with her agitation.

"Try to remember," Norah urged, and placed her card in the silver salver beside the keyboard. "Then call me. It's important."

Norah had parked down the block from Mary Ruth's building. For the singer's benefit, in case she should be watching, she got into the car and drove off—around the corner to another parking place. She came back on foot, found a spot in a doorway across the street where she was hidden from view but could observe the building entrance. Half an hour passed, then another half hour. Norah was debating the advisability of slipping to the phone booth on the corner and calling the squad for someone to take over the surveillance, when a radio cab pulled up. Minutes later, Mary Ruth Rae came out. She had a large suitcase and a tote. The driver placed both bags in the trunk while she got into the back seat. It was Norah's chance to leave the doorway and go around the corner to her car. She got into it as the cab crossed Park Avenue. Fortunately, Sixty-sixth was also eastbound so she could run parallel and pick it up on Lexington. She followed to Second where the cab turned and joined the lane to the lower level of the Queensboro Bridge.

From then on there was little chance of being spotted. Not that Mary Ruth appeared nervous; she hadn't looked back once. Norah was the one who kept checking her rearview mirror, watching the lanes around her. She was worried that someone besides herself might be following the singer. The heavy traffic that camouflaged her Volvo so well did the same for whoever else might be part of the tail. So, she might as well relax, Norah thought, at least till they got to La Guardia or Kennedy Airport.

It turned out to be Kennedy and the TWA terminal. Norah parked in a restricted area, flashed her open shield case at the attendant, and ran. She sprinted for the main waiting area and stopped abruptly when she saw Mary Ruth Rae's flaming hair like a beacon at the far end of the check-in counter. Norah could afford to hang back, even to take a look around at the crowd. It seemed to be the usual assortment of travelers, some excited, some bored; of friends seeing them off or waiting to welcome them home. As far as Norah could tell, no one had a particular interest in the redhead. Nevertheless, she kept watching and maintained her distance till the ticket was written, the bag checked through, and Mary Ruth Rae headed in the direction of the departure gates.

Norah quickened her pace so as to pass her unobserved and then stepped in front of her.

"You didn't tell me you were planning to leave town, Ms. Rae."

The singer gasped.

"You should have told me."

"It was sudden. My mother . . . I'm going to visit my mother. She's sick."

"I'm sorry to hear that. What's wrong with her?"

"Heart condition. She hasn't been well for a long time."

"You said you were expecting your voice coach."

"I was, but I canceled. I told her I'd be away for a couple of weeks. Actually, I'd been meaning to visit my mom . . ." Her voice trailed off.

"And this seemed like a good time to go?"

"Exactly. Yes." From defensive, the redhead turned positive. "I felt like getting away for a couple of weeks. Why not? You didn't tell me not to. You didn't tell me I had to stay." A sudden doubt assailed her. "You're not going to tell me I can't go, are you? You can't do that."

"What are you running away from, Mary Ruth?" Norah asked. "What are you afraid of?"

"Nothing. I don't know what you're talking about. I'm

going to visit my mother in Jacksonville. You can't stop me."

"I thought you said you came from Claymore, West Virginia."

"That's right. When my pa died, Ma moved in with her sister in Jacksonville."

"What are you afraid of, Mary Ruth?" Norah asked again. "Tell me about it. I can help you. I want to help you."

The young woman wavered. Norah could sense her uncertainty. She needed to unburden herself and Norah almost held her breath so as not to disturb the precarious balance.

"I don't need any help."

She said it firmly and she meant it, for the moment at least, Norah thought. She asked "Does it have to do with the death of Peter Hines?"

"All I know about Peter's death is what you told me," Mary Ruth replied. Her lips were twitching.

"I can protect you," Norah assured her. "How about Imogene Davies? Does it have anything to do with her?"

"I haven't seen Imo in six months, not since I moved out of her place. I told Sergeant Arenas. I told him she was a very emotional, volatile person. She had big highs and low lows. She could have jumped out the window." Now, unexpectedly, Mary Ruth did looked around, nervously. "I hate to think she did. I hate to think what her emotional state must have been if she did that. I'm sorry for her, but it wasn't my fault and I don't know anything about it. So please, leave me alone. Just leave me alone."

"You can't just walk away from this, Mary Ruth."

But the redhead did just that. She turned her back on Norah Mulcahaney and with firm, deliberate steps started for the long tunnel to the departure area.

"Will you be coming back?" Norah called out.

That stopped her and made her turn around. "Of course." She was surprised at the question.

"When?" Norah challenged.

Their eyes met.

"When my mother feels better."

And Norah had to let it go at that.

CHAPTER FIFTEEN

Norah watched as the flamboyant redhead passed through the security check and disappeared into the jetway leading to the aircraft. The moment Mary Ruth had heard about Hines's death, her manner had changed. Up to that point she'd been cautious but not uncooperative. Then reserve turned to fear. Obviously she'd been scared. The rush to the airport was proof enough, thought Norah as she stood to one side and watched the last-minute passengers dash for the gate.

Should she have stopped the singer even if it meant arresting her? There were no grounds for an arrest, but that wouldn't have mattered, since the primary purpose to stop her from leaving would have been served. Then what? Norah had promised protection and she would have made good on the promise even if it meant taking the duty herself. But how long could she have provided it? Protection was always a matter of time—how many man-hours you could afford. Once the guards were removed, the subject became as vulnerable as before. No, at this stage, it was best for Mary Ruth Rae to go, Norah thought as she continued to scrutinize the stragglers.

The last one, a red-faced, overweight man in a flapping black raincoat and carrying an attaché case entered the passenger area and the gate closed behind him. Something about the man wasn't right. The case was too new, too expensive; it didn't go with the rest of him. She was being overly suspicious, Norah chided herself, too anxious. By running away like this, Mary Ruth Rae was sending a clear message that she intended to keep her mouth shut.

The question was: For whom was it intended?

As soon as Norah walked into the squad room, Art Potts waved her over.

"He wants you." They both knew whom he meant. "Inspector Felix called. Also, Doc Worgan. He says he was returning your call. Felix didn't say what he wanted."

Norah sighed; she knew, of course. "I'll check Doc first."

"Don't be too long," he warned.

"I won't."

Norah ducked into her office. Art Potts, Captain Jacoby's executive officer, acted as a buffer between the sometimes irascible commander and the men and women under him. If Manny Jacoby had been at the point of exploding, Art would have advised her to go straight in. Nevertheless, Norah followed his advice and didn't waste any time placing her call to the medical examiner. She was lucky enough to get straight through.

"It's Norah, Phil. I wanted to know if you had a cause of death on Peter Hines yet."

"You know what time it was when we got him."

"Yes, but . . ."

"Dr. Yost is conducting the autopsy now. He's a good man."

"I know that. I'm not suggesting otherwise, but something about the case doesn't feel right."

"What?"

"That he died as the result of the beating."

"You want me to take a look?"

"I'd appreciate it."

Art Potts opened the door and put his head in. "Sorry, Norah, I had to tell him you were back. He wants you—*forthwith.*"

*   *   *

"Where've you been?" Captain Jacoby demanded.

"Kennedy Airport."

Clearly, the answer was unexpected. "Doing what?"

"Catching up with a witness. Mary Ruth Rae. She's a singer, protégée of Gilda Valente. She's the one who put us on to Hines. She said she was going to visit her sick mother in Jacksonville."

"So?"

"She lied to Ferdi about not knowing where Hines was. I don't think that's all she was holding back."

"And you let her go?"

"I couldn't stop her," Norah flared, for the very reason that she still felt she should somehow have stopped Mary Ruth.

Emmanuel Jacoby, though he appeared to be totally immersed in the administrative details of his command, in fact knew his people very well. He understood Norah's dissatisfaction. "As long as you can put your hand on her if you need her." He paused. "You do know where she is?"

"I know where she said she was going."

Jacoby took his feet off the low stool and, planting them firmly on the floor, leaned forward across the desk. "This isn't like you, Lieutenant."

"She's booked for Jacksonville. I saw her on to the plane and waited till the gate closed. But there's no guarantee she'll stay there."

Once a thing was done, for good or ill, as far as Manny Jacoby was concerned, it was over. He accepted it and went on. "You figure the Hines homicide was a gangland job and linked to the Valente case."

"It's linked, but I'm waiting for the autopsy report."

Jacoby's jet button eyes got smaller. "What do you expect the autopsy will turn up?"

Norah bit her lip. "I'm not sure. The kind of beating he got is usually intended as punishment or warning or both. It bothers me that it was fatal."

"So, they miscalculated."

"Being Valente's people, I doubt that."

Jacoby didn't argue; he had another concern. "Reporters have been calling all morning. What are you going to tell them?"

This is it, Norah thought, the moment she'd been preparing for and dreading. She had intended to announce her decision to Jim Felix first, but why wait? After all, Manny Jacoby was her commanding officer. He was the one to whom she should report. And, since her mind was made up, she might as well get it over.

"Captain, I'm not taking on any more PR assignments."

"I haven't been informed. Who said so? Who decided?"

"Nobody. Me. I did. I'm through with it. I've had enough."

"Have you talked to Inspector Felix? Or Chief Deland?"

"I'm reporting to you, sir. I'm asking to be relieved of the PR duty, Captain." Manny Jacoby was a stickler for following the chain of command, but he was not the one who had made the assignment. "I'd appreciate it, sir, if you'd speak to the inspector or the chief in my behalf." Even that was putting him in an awkward position.

"I thought you were enjoying it."

She was dismayed that even he had noticed. "Yes, sir, I was. Too much, as it turns out. I've been appearing on television, going to fancy restaurants, the theater, sitting on the dais and giving speeches on police work. The real police work is not getting my full attention."

"You're doing what the department needs you to do, Lieutenant. There are other detectives here, good ones. You are not indispensable."

Norah could feel herself blushing. "I didn't mean to suggest that, Captain. But I am in charge of the homicide squad and we've got two complex and very sensitive investigations ongoing. Stefanie Altman's case is scheduled to go to the grand jury next Monday. Despite the postponement, we're nowhere near ready. As for the Valente case, we haven't even scratched the surface and the complications keep piling up. There's no question in my mind that Peter Hines was killed because of his relationship with Mrs. Valente, but all we know for sure at this point is that he was a protégé of hers—at one time. So were Imogene Davies and Mary Ruth Rae. Could be there were others. If so, we'd better find them. Soon."

She paused. "So, unless the chief wants to relieve me of the command, I'm going back to work and do the job the way I see it or not at all."

"Is that a threat, Lieutenant?" Jacoby asked. "I wouldn't make it if I were you, not unless you're prepared to go through with it."

Norah frowned. Jacoby and the brass wanted her to be a glamorized spokeswoman and role model for the department. Randall Tye saw her as a new kind of personality he could groom and commercialize. All she wanted was to get back to reality and be the only thing she'd ever wanted to be—a good police officer.

"I'm sorry, Captain. I didn't mean it to sound like a threat." She hesitated; she agonized; she couldn't take it back. "I intend to do the job I was sworn in to do."

She waited a couple of moments, but Manny Jacoby had nothing more to say to her—for now—so she turned and walked out.

Back in her own office, Norah realized she was shaking. Manny Jacoby would stand by her; she was sure of it. So would Jim Felix. But Chief Deland might not be so understanding. He couldn't take her rank from her, she'd earned that through civil service, but he could flop her back into uniform and assign her somewhere else—Traffic, Internal Affairs, give her desk duty. The least she could expect was a reprimand. She wasn't disposed to accept that meekly. While she sat staring at the family pictures on her wall imagining what might happen and what she could do about it, she was suddenly ashamed. She had told Jacoby that all she wanted was to get back to doing regular detective work. So she ought to get out there and do it. Investigate. Solve something. *Show them how good you really are!*

* * *

Stefanie Altman was seated at a desk about halfway into the narrow bookshop. From there she could both see and be seen through the plate glass of the display window. She was trying to follow a normal routine, but the quick look up, the instinctive flinch before she assured herself the visitor presented no threat and she released the lock to admit her, were indications she was having a hard time of it.

"Lieutenant Mulcahaney. What can I do for you?"

She appeared listless, neither pleased nor displeased by Norah's visit.

"How are you feeling?"

Stefanie Altman shrugged. "I'm about to be indicted for murder. How should I feel?"

"I'd like to go over your story once more, Ms. Altman."

"Why? What else is there to know? Haven't your detectives dug up enough? Isn't the district attorney satisfied?"

"I don't work for the district attorney. I'm not on his squad."

"So who do you work for?" Stefie Altman demanded.

Norah had no immediate answer. She had never asked herself that question. "You're the public. I work for you."

"I don't want your help. Thank you very much."

"Ms. Altman . . ."

"Look, he raped me once. We were on a date; that's what it was supposed to be. He took me home and then forced his way into the apartment after me. He was on me before I knew what was happening. I tried to push him off. I screamed. It was a hot August night and the windows were open but nobody came. He had a bet on it. Did you know that? So he won his bet. This last time he brought his buddies with him. I didn't bother to scream. I'd already learned not to look for help from anybody but myself. It was either shoot or let the three of them get on me. I shot in self-defense. Why can't anybody accept that?"

"You admit that you did know Frank Beech before?"

"Yes, yes. Certainly, I admit it."

"You must see that your prior knowledge of Beech is crucial to the case."

"I didn't shoot him because I knew he was Frank Beech. I shot him because I was afraid. I didn't recognize him," Stefie Altman insisted. "I didn't know who he was till after I shot him. I swear."

"Exactly when was that?" Norah asked.

"After I shot him. After he was down. After the other two had run away."

"You'll have to be more precise."

The girl sighed wearily and frowned as she tried to re-create the exact sequence. "I fired. He staggered back a step or so—at the impact, I suppose. Then half turning, he fell to his knees, and tumbled down the stairs and across the sidewalk where he finally lay still. The men with him stayed at the bottom of the steps the whole time. One of them, the one who had a ski mask on like Beech's, yelled at me. *'You shot him! Bitch! Bitch! You'll be sorry!'* I thought they were going to come after me, so I fired again. I fired over their heads. I didn't want to hit either one. I just wanted them to go away."

"But you did hit Carl Pesrow in the leg."

"I know. I'm sorry. I didn't mean to."

"All right. Go on."

"When I was sure they were gone, I went down the steps to see what I could do for the man in the street. I knelt beside him. The front of his jacket was soaked with blood. Soaked. I was horrified. He didn't move. I couldn't believe he was dead. I couldn't believe it. I hadn't meant to kill him, just to stop him. That's the truth," Stefanie Altman pleaded. "Nobody believes it," she groaned. "What's the use?"

"I would like to believe you," Norah said softly.

"You don't care." Stefanie Altman shook her head. "When I first saw you on Monday night, I was so glad. I thought, being a woman, you'd understand. I expected you to be on my side."

"I told you then I was on the side of the truth. You didn't tell me the truth, Stefanie. You weren't honest with me or with any of the police you talked to that night or since."

"I was afraid. I was afraid that if I admitted knowing Frank Beech, that he'd attacked me once before, you'd think I shot him intending to kill him in revenge. And I was right. That's what everybody thinks."

"Let's forget about that for now," Norah suggested. "I want you to tell me exactly what happened from the time the other two men fled and you went down to look at Beech. Did you feel for a pulse or check to see if he was still breathing?"

"I did, yes," the girl responded eagerly. "But I couldn't tell, not with the ski mask. It had a slit for the eyes, but covered the nose and mouth. So I had to get it off him. I rolled it up from his neck and then pulled it the rest of the way over the top of his head. That was when I recognized him. That was when I knew exactly how this whole thing would turn out."

"Didn't it strike you as a coincidence for Beech to just happen to choose you to mug?"

"All I thought about was what to tell the police."

It rang true. Norah expelled a soft, barely perceptible sigh. So far the instinct that had brought her here was proving valid. "Did he recognize you?"

Stefanie Altman considered. "I wasn't aware that he did."

Again, the right answer. "And the knife?"

The girl hung her head.

"No knife? You lied about that, too."

"I thought people would be more likely to believe the threat if I said that he had a knife."

It would turn out to be a black mark against her, Norah thought. "Let's go back to the evening of the thirtieth just before the attack. You closed the store early."

Stefie nodded, glad to be on what she considered safe ground. "There were no customers and not likely to be any on such a night."

"Timothy Kampel came by. He wanted to see you home, but you turned him down."

"He dropped by on his way to work," she corrected. "He invited me to the performance at the Met—he works in the restaurant there, but you know that. The house would be half empty; he'd have no trouble getting me in."

"You don't like opera?"

"I do. A lot, but I was tired. I don't often have the chance to get home before ten."

"So then Timothy offered to see you home?" The girl nodded. "Was the street busy when you locked up? Were there a lot of people around?"

"I didn't pay attention. Usually, at that hour there's not much activity. That afternoon, what with the snow . . . No, I don't think there were any passersby."

"You've had four robberies in the past three months. I would think you'd be extremely watchful, especially coming and going."

"I was. I am. But Timothy was with me."

"Why didn't you let him take you all the way home?"

"I didn't want him to be late for work. And I didn't think it was necessary." She paused. "I didn't think muggers would be out in that kind of weather."

Norah got up, went to the door, then signaled Stefanie to release the lock for her. She stepped outside. The block was predominantly residential, consisting of what had once been private townhouses, now converted to apartments. They were set well back from the street and most had high stoops and basement entrances tucked underneath. Ideal for loitering, Norah thought, and went back inside.

"When did you first notice you were being followed?"

"After Timothy and I parted. At the corner of Columbus and Seventieth."

"And you're sure the men you saw on that corner were the same ones who followed you to your home and then accosted you?"

Stefanie Altman wasn't clear about what Norah was after, but she did finally understand that Norah was trying to help. Her big myopic eyes filled and her voice trembled.

"There was nobody else out."

* * *

Three men, Norah thought: the first, dead; the second, transformed from criminal to victim; the third, missing. Still missing. Damn.

Norah sat at her desk in the fading afternoon light, staring at nothing. According to Carl Pesrow, he and Beech had met and joined forces with that man, "Dan," at the Acme Employment Agency on the morning of the blizzard. Simon Wyler had established that there were forty-nine job applicants there and that thirty had been sent out. Of the nineteen left, Beech and Pesrow were two. He had traced and interrogated every one of the other seventeen—without result. As for the carpet warehouse, Beech and Pesrow and "Dan" got there late, after the jobs were filled, so they hadn't even made out applications. There had been nothing for Wyler to follow up.

She continued to sit and stare blankly. Pesrow's story led to a dead end. He claimed he was anxious to have the third man found because he would corroborate his testimony. But suppose, in fact, the third man's evidence would do the opposite? Suppose it would confirm Altman's version? Pesrow couldn't deny "Dan's" existence, but he could mislead and confuse the investigation just enough so that he wouldn't be found. Dismay numbed Norah. She should have seen it before, long ago. That she hadn't only indicated how thoroughly distracted she'd been playing the celebrity. She thought of the time and manpower wasted and was filled with anger and frustration. Resolutely, she set her emotions aside and tried to reason it out.

Norah had a feeling that Pesrow hadn't lied so much as twisted the truth. He and Beech had been at the Acme Agency—it was a proven fact—but suppose they hadn't met "Dan" there? Suppose they'd met him at the warehouse? An obstacle arose immediately. If Beech and Pesrow hadn't met the unknown at Acme, how had they found out about the jobs at the warehouse? None of the seventeen applicants Wyler had interviewed had known anything about that. She shifted in her chair. Maybe . . .

The warehouse number was in Wyler's report. She found it, picked up the phone, and dialed.

It was four-thirty on Friday afternoon and the regular manager, the man who had been there on Monday, was gone, but the night manager was able to answer her question.

"No, we didn't run an ad," he told Norah. "And we don't hire anybody off the street. Strict company policy. We have valuable merchandise lying around and we have to make sure the people we hire are trustworthy. We rely on the agency to check them out before sending them to us. Why don't you contact Elite, Lieutenant?"

"I thought you got your people from Acme?"

"No, Lieutenant. The Elite Agency. We have a contract with them. We've never used anybody else."

It was nearly five. The grand-jury hearing of the Altman case was scheduled for Monday. She could hardly hope for another postponement, Norah thought as she listened to the repeated ringing at Elite and prayed they hadn't closed yet. On the fourth peal, she heard the click as the answering machine cut in and her heart sank. Then a voice overrode the recording.

"Elite Office and Industrial Agency. Mrs. Auerbach. May I help you?"

Joan Auerbach, Elite's office manager, agreed to wait till Norah got there. She was middle-aged, comfortably overweight, efficient. Once the situation was explained, she was eager to cooperate and it didn't take long for her to compile a list of the men who had applied for work on the morning of the thirtieth. It included Beech and Pesrow, but they had come in too late to be sent on the warehouse job.

"In that case how could they have found out about it?"

Mrs. Auerbach shrugged. "Maybe from somebody here who had been passed over."

She had no idea who that might be, nor did any of the staff who had been curious enough to wait along with her. Of the handful of clients still on the benches, four had been present on that particular morning. Norah spoke to each one, but they couldn't tell her anything. These men were part of the chronically unemployed; their attention was turned within; they had no interest in anything outside themselves.

So, another dead end. Yet the feeling that the answer was within her grasp persisted.

"Mrs. Auerbach, you said Beech and Pesrow might have learned about the warehouse jobs from somebody here who had been passed over . . ." She was still groping. "Could that include any of your regulars?"

"Certainly."

"I don't suppose they would have filled out an employment application that day?"

"No, they'd just sign the daily sheet."

The two women looked at each other. Norah was almost afraid to ask.

"You do still have the sheet?"

Within minutes, thanks to the efficiency of Joan Auerbach and the miracle of the computer, Norah had a copy. It consisted of twenty-two names. Twenty-two regular clients of the Elite Agency to be tracked down and interrogated. At least their addresses were on file. Between herself, Wyler, Tedesco, and Ochs, they should be able to do it. They should finally find the missing witness.

And they did—with one day to spare. To be precise, it was Simon Wyler who located him early on Sunday. He was not at all what any of them had expected.

"I think he's actually glad we found him," Wyler reported. "His conscience has been bothering him because he didn't come forward."

"Good."

"But he doesn't want his wife or his sons to know. And he also doesn't want anybody at his regular job to find out."

"What did you tell him?"

"That we couldn't make any promises, but we'd try to respect his confidence."

Norah nodded.

CHAPTER SIXTEEN

Wyler brought Daniel Roskoff in that Sunday afternoon. Norah had him put into one of the interrogation rooms and then let him wait. Not too long—she didn't want him to get overly nervous—only long enough to give him a taste of what being locked up felt like.

"Hello, Mr. Roskoff. I'm Lieutenant Mulcahaney and you know Detective Wyler," she said as the two of them entered. She sat at the table across from the witness and Wyler took a position beside the door. As she placed the sheaf of papers she'd brought with her carefully in front of her, Norah studied Roskoff. He was in his mid-fifties; a stolid, gray man, dressed in what she assumed was his best, a navy three-piece suit. Hat in hand, he had risen to his feet when she came in.

"Please, sit, Mr. Roskoff," she said, and opened the file. "I see that you work at the Marlboro House, an apartment building on West End Avenue, as a doorman and that you've been there thirty-one years."

"Thirty-three, ma'am," Roskoff corrected deferentially.

Beech and Pesrow could be characterized as on the edge of vagrancy, Norah thought; this man was the exact opposite. She nodded, acknowledging the error. "That's a very long time."

"Yes, ma'am. They're good people to work for."

"The pay can't be that good, not if you have to moon-light."

"I've got a son in medical school and another starting college."

"I see." Again, Norah consulted the papers in front of her. "This is a very serious business, Mr. Roskoff. You have a good work record both with your primary employ-ers and also with the Elite Agency. Both cite you as reli-able and honest. Now suddenly you're involved in what appears to have been attempted robbery."

Norah waited for Roskoff to protest, to excuse himself, to explain. He didn't.

"A robbery that went bad and got one of the perpetra-tors killed and the other wounded."

Roskoff sighed heavily.

"Has Detective Wyler read you your rights? And do you understand those rights as he explained them to you?"

"Yes, ma'am."

"Very well. I want to know exactly what happened, Mr. Roskoff. You have an obligation to the man who was killed and to the woman who shot him to tell the truth. If you lie, you'll only complicate matters and make it a lot worse for yourself."

"Yes, ma'am. I'll tell you everything. Believe me, I've never been involved in anything like this before. I'm not much of a drinker. That was part of the problem. We were drinking and . . ."

"Let's start at the beginning," Norah said. "When and how did you meet Frank Beech and Carl Pesrow?"

The witness cast a look at Wyler; he'd told it all, the look said, but patiently Roskoff told it again. "We met at the Elite Agency. It was slow—right after Thanksgiving there's usually a lull, then it picks up closer to Christmas—the only call that morning was for porters and warehousemen at this big carpet place up here on Broadway. That involved a lot of lifting and hauling—too heavy for me; I've got a heart condition. So, I waited around to see if anything else might come in. While I waited, Frank and Carl showed up and decided to hang around too. We got to talking. You know how it is. I mentioned the warehouse and they decided they might as well go up there and try for it. I went with them."

"I thought you said the work was too much for you?"

"Sometimes when they take on a lot of extra blue-collar people, say for a big sale, they end up needing clerical help too." He shrugged. "I was at loose ends. I had nothing else to do."

Norah nodded. "Go on."

"Anyway, it didn't matter because by the time we got there, the jobs were gone and by then so was the morning. Ordinarily, I would have called it a day and gone home for lunch, but the guys suggested a beer. They were friendly, easy to talk to; good guys, at least I thought so. We were having some laughs. It was a long time since I'd had a few beers and a few laughs with the guys. So I went along."

He paused and raised his eyes to Norah. Surprisingly gentle they were. An old dog's trusting eyes, she thought, and suddenly felt sorry for the tired old man.

"Well, one beer led to the next and then we were out of money, most of it mine, and we still hadn't eaten. It was well into the afternoon, I'm not sure about the exact time, but I knew I should finally be going home. Frank wouldn't hear of it. He said he wanted to pay me back and he knew where he could get some money. He had a girlfriend in the neighborhood and she would give him whatever he wanted. It wasn't far, he said. To be honest, I would have been glad to get my money."

"You have no idea of the time?" Norah asked.

"I can only tell you it was snowing fairly heavily by then. One more block, Frank kept saying, just one more. We turned the corner on Seventieth, I think, I'm not sure, and we stopped in front of this little bookstore in the basement. There was this girl inside but she had a man with her. Frank said we should wait till she was alone. So we got under one of the stoops for shelter. It was snowing hard and it was cold." He huddled in on himself, remembering.

Norah nodded encouragingly. Her heart was beating fast. She cast a look at Wyler, who returned it with suppressed excitement.

"But the man didn't leave. The girl put on a coat and galoshes, turned out the lights, and the two of them came out together. She locked up and they went over to Columbus and started uptown. We followed. I don't know why. I didn't ask. It seemed . . . like some kind of game. Actually, I was feeling my drinks . . ." His voice trailed off.

"Mr. Roskoff?" Norah recalled him.

"Yes, yes. After a couple of blocks, the man and the girl parted and we closed in on the girl. We weren't trying to hide anymore. Frank and Carl pulled out ski masks from their pockets and put them on. That was a shock to me. They were going to rip her off! I couldn't believe it. I didn't want to believe it, but it was obvious that she wasn't an old friend and they weren't just going to ask her to help them out with a few dollars."

No wonder Pesrow hadn't wanted the old man found, Norah thought.

"I didn't know what to do," the old man went on. "I realize now I should have yelled to the girl, warned her, but I just kept tagging along. I could tell from the way the girl was looking back over her shoulder that she knew she was being followed and she was scared, but I honestly didn't think anything really bad was going to happen—not till she turned the corner, got to her building, and climbed the stairs. By then, Frank was right behind her. He climbed the stairs after her. She was so scared she dropped her keys in the snow. He picked them up.

" 'How much will you give me for the keys?' he demanded. He was laughing. So was Carl. The girl was terrified.

" 'How much?' Beech went on. 'How much, sweetheart? Want me to open the door for you? Want me to take you inside?' He was laughing like a maniac."

That was a new line, one Norah hadn't heard before, nor had it appeared in either Stefanie Altman's statement nor Pesrow's. She didn't challenge it. Daniel Roskoff was reliving a nightmare that unfortunately had happened. She would not interrupt him.

"The girl started to cry and to plead that she had no money. 'Go away,' she kept saying. 'Go away. Leave me alone. I have no money.' Then she pulled the gun out of her coat pocket. I froze. We all did.

"She pointed the gun at Frank, but her hand was shaking. I remember thinking that with her hand shaking like that she might not be able to pull the trigger. I thought it was my chance to run, but my legs wouldn't move. Then Beech screamed, 'No, don't shoot. For God's sake, Stefie, don't shoot!'

"But she did shoot. Beech fell to his knees, stayed like that for a couple of seconds, then tumbled down the steps to the street." Roskoff sighed. "Then we ran. No, no, wait. I told her she should call an ambulance. Yes, I told her that. And Carl screamed something at her. Then she fired at us. So then we ran and kept going till we turned the corner."

He stopped. Norah waited. He was finished.

"Your story differs in one detail from the account Mr. Pesrow and Ms. Altman gave us," Norah told him.

"That's the way I remember it."

"We'll go over it just once more," Norah told him quietly. "Let's start just before Ms. Altman pulled the gun. What were your positions?"

"Frank was on the landing facing her. Carl and I were at the bottom of the steps. He was on my left."

"You had a clear view?"

"Yes."

"Ms. Altman was holding the gun on Beech, not on you or Pesrow?"

"That's right. He was the one up there with her, threatening."

"Not taunting?"

Roskoff hesitated. "Both."

"And demanding money?"

"Yes."

"Once more then, Mr. Roskoff, please. What did Ms. Altman say?"

He closed his eyes in concentration. "She said: 'I have no money. Go away. Leave me alone.' "

"And he said?"

" 'No, don't shoot. For God's sake, Stefie, don't shoot!' "

"You're sure?"

Roskoff opened his eyes and in them Norah saw the realization of just what he was committing himself to.

"Yes, ma'am. Those were his exact words."

CHAPTER
SEVENTEEN

"It's a standoff," Wyler said as they left the interrogation room. "At the very best."

"Maybe not." Norah was thoughtful. "Actually, it's a matter of interpretation."

"Well, we know how the DA will interpret it," Wyler pointed out.

"What counts is how the grand jury sees it," she answered. "It might be helpful to make sure the ADA knows what the options are."

It was late that Sunday night when Norah finally was able to reach the ADA in charge of the Altman case. Reluctantly, John Douvas agreed to see her in his office early Monday morning before going to court.

John Douvas was twenty-eight, thin, with curly light brown hair and green eyes and well-chiseled features. Women were immediately attracted to him, but he was interested only in his work. No matter how unusual, shocking, dramatic, Douvas by his methodical cataloguing could reduce it to routine. He knew only one way to proceed—doggedly. There were over 250 assistants to the district attorney of New York. By dint of strict adherence to procedure and sacrifice of any personal interests, Douvas had in his four years on the job reached the top ten.

To go higher would require a flair and a willingness to take risks of which so far he had shown no indication.

Norah handed him Daniel Roskoff's signed deposition and waited while he studied it. He took his time and she was glad that he did. Finished, he looked up and she girded herself for the inevitable challenges and arguments. But he merely sighed and went back to the beginning of the document and read it through once more.

Douvas's office was one of a series of partitioned cubicles within a large room. The noise and clatter of the other cages and of the big central area couldn't be kept out. It didn't bother Douvas. He had the habit of absolute concentration that was essential to getting the work done, Norah thought, respecting him for it, and settled back in the single visitor's chair wedged between the filing cabinet and the wall to wait patiently. At least he wasn't dismissing the testimony.

"It's a matter of interpretation," Douvas said.

She nodded. "I agree."

"That's a pleasant surprise. I was afraid we were headed for a confrontation. You have a reputation for being . . ."

"Stubborn?" Norah smiled. "Only when I'm right."

"I thought we just agreed . . ."

"That it's a matter of interpretation—yes. Not that we see it the same way. I don't believe you've weighed all the possibilities, Mr. Douvas. You haven't had time."

"I assure you, Lieutenant, I understand the situation. I have judged this statement purely on its merits. Which, I'm afraid, you have not. You do have a tendency to be sympathetic and to favor the victim."

"Ah!" She caught him up instantly. "You do admit that Stefanie Altman is the victim."

"No. You see her as the victim and your logic proceeds from that premise and is therefore flawed."

Norah stifled a sigh. "Mr. Douvas, John—may I call you John? Frank Beech and Carl Pesrow were carrying ski masks. Altman stated both men were wearing them and now Roskoff confirms it. Doesn't the fact that they had ski masks handy suggest they had used them in previous forays? It's as good as finding burglar's tools on them."

"It would be if it hadn't been snowing."

"It wasn't snowing when they left Staten Island that morning. If you expect anybody to believe that Beech and Pesrow went out with ski masks in their pockets because of the weather forecast but without caps, or gloves, or boots—fine, but how do you explain that they weren't wearing the masks when Altman first observed them? They were wearing them when they caught up with her at the steps of her house. Roskoff agrees that's the way it was."

"How did Frank Beech know where to find Altman? How did he know she'd bought the bookstore?" Douvas countered.

"He kept track of her. He got fired because of her and he was looking to pay her back."

"He didn't give a damn about that job, or any job," the ADA scoffed.

"That's right," Norah agreed. "But she'd made him look bad in front of his buddies. He was supposed to be a lover, not a rapist."

"All right, I'll accept that. I'll accept that the encounter was no happenstance, that Beech deliberately sought out Stefanie Altman, that he led Pesrow and Roskoff to Altman's store and waited for her to come out, that he then followed her along with his companions with the intent of getting money from her."

It was too easy, Norah thought. Knowing Douvas's reputation, she couldn't believe that he would capitulate so easily. What had she missed?

"I'll agree that Beech was wearing the ski mask when he accosted Altman and that his mouth was covered so as to muffle and distort his voice. I'll even agree that under the conditions of weather, not having had contact with Beech in over a year, she was not likely to recognize his voice, distorted or not. However, she was still emotionally damaged by the rape she had suffered at his hands. She has admitted that more than being robbed or injured, she feared sexual assault. Once he called out her name, once he shouted, *"Stefie!"* she had to know who he was and remember the terrible violation he had inflicted on her. She shot him knowing who he was and exactly what she was doing. Please, don't waste time arguing, Lieutenant. You won't get me to change my mind."

"I won't try."

"Good."

"I'm willing to assume, for the moment, that Stefanie Altman did, in fact, recognize Frank Beech when he called out her name. That in that terrible moment her worst fears were confirmed. If she knew who he was, she also knew he wouldn't be satisfied with money no matter how much she might be able to turn over. If she knew Beech, then she also knew what he was capable of doing to her—everything he had done the first time—and more. Recognizing him, she had every reason and justification to shoot. If she knew him, then she certainly shot in self-defense."

Douvas scowled. He ran his long fingers through his lank hair. "We're both building on the testimony of one witness who may or may not be mistaken."

"But who can't be ignored."

"There's no question of ignoring him." He glared. "I'll examine Roskoff, of course. It means postponing this afternoon's hearing, but it can't be helped."

Norah's heart surged.

"I wish you'd turned him sooner," Douvas complained. "I've already spent too much time on this case."

"I wish we had too."

"Well, I understand, Lieutenant. You've been busy on other matters."

That stung. The DA's office had a special squad of detectives to conduct investigations solely for the prosecutor. Douvas could have ordered a search for the missing third man, if he'd been honestly interested in getting the truth. It was on the tip of her tongue to say so, but she didn't. She waited till she'd cooled down a little.

"I've made quite a few friends in the entertainment

business lately, John. If you want to go on TV I can probably fix it for you. Give me a call." She got up.

"Thanks, Norah; that won't be necessary. I'll get all the media exposure I want trying this case."

She shouldn't have said it, Norah thought. Damn. Now he was as unyielding as before.

"Why are you so determined to convict Stefanie Altman?" she asked in frustration.

"Why are you so determined to clear her?"

CHAPTER EIGHTEEN

Since Friday when she'd made her decision to resign from the PR assignments and had informed Captain Jacoby of her intent, Norah had spent a minimum of time in her office, slipping in and out as unobtrusively as possible. On each occasion, she expected and dreaded the order to report to Chief Deland or Inspector Felix. But nothing happened. Maybe Jacoby hadn't been able to reach the chief or the inspector? Or maybe he hadn't tried? Was that possible? Norah wondered. It was Manny Jacoby's policy to get rid of unpleasant tasks quickly to get out from under onerous responsibility. So he was buying her a little extra time, Norah thought with a surge of surprise and gratitude. The best way to thank him was to use it well.

"Norah . . ."

Art Potts called to her just as she reached her door.

She sighed and stopped. "What's up?" She knew perfectly well.

"Doc Worgan's been trying to get you. He left a number. It's on your desk."

"Oh?" She was relieved and Potts knew it. "Thanks, Art." They shared a smile before she went inside.

Before even taking off her coat, she dialed the number. "Dr. Worgan, please. Lieutenant Mulcahaney calling."

"Hold the line, Lieutenant."

The cacophany of voices in the background and the length of time she waited were indications that she had reached a crime scene and that Phil Worgan was at work. His willingness to be interrupted meant he had something important.

Worgan came on. "You asked me to check on the cause of death in the Hines case. It was suffocation."

"Suffocation?"

"Right. There are no marks on his throat to indicate he was strangled. I figure that after the beating he was either unconscious or close to it. All anybody had to do was pick up a pillow and hold it over his face." He paused. "Okay, Norah?"

"How about time of death?"

"Can't say precisely. Not yet. If you remember, the place was very cold."

She did remember; she'd been cold even in her fur coat.

"We'll be analyzing the stomach contents and that may tell us what we want to know. I've got to get back, now."

"Sure. Thanks, Phil. Thanks very much." She hung up.

So her hunch had been right, Norah thought, and Peter Hines did not die as a direct result of the beating. Valente was not responsible, not directly; suffocation was not the usual MO for a mob rubout. That meant there was another perpetrator. When Valente's thugs left, someone came after them. Norah took off her vinyl storm coat and hung it in the locker. She sat down, sliding low on her spine, legs stretched out under the desk, and looked up at the ceiling.

Had the killer walked in and found Hines semiconscious by chance? Or did he know ahead of time that Hines would be worked over?

CHAPTER NINETEEN

It was time to set half-formed notions aside and start fresh. Norah got a pad out of her drawer and wrote: *Gilda Valente, Imogene Davies, Peter Hines:* the three victims. Next, she put down: *Alibis.* Under that she listed:

Dario Valente.

The *capo's* alibi for his wife's death was unshakable. Norah had seen for herself his condition when he returned to the city. It couldn't have been faked. As for his alibis for the time of Imogene Davies's and Peter Hines's deaths, his secretary, Salvatore Nunzio, stated they had been together in the penthouse office, working. Norah had no doubt that if necessary Valente could produce any number of others to vouch for him. It wouldn't be necessary. The first alibi was more than enough.

What about the private and confidential secretary, she asked herself, and wrote:

Salvatore Nunzio.

He claimed to have been playing poker with four buddies on the night his boss's wife drowned in her penthouse swimming pool. His friends backed him. As far as Norah was concerned it didn't mean much; their testimonies could be bought and paid for. With regard to the other two murders, Nunzio's alibi for his boss served as an alibi for himself. That brought up the question of motive.

Could there have been an illicit relationship between Salvatore Nunzio, young and good-looking, and his boss's young and beautiful wife? Dangerous. Extremely. For both of them. So much so that Norah had written it off right at the start, but she was forced to reconsider.

Could Nunzio have been the father of the child Gilda was carrying? If she had threatened to tell her husband, that would have been a compelling reason to silence her permanently. Except that, whether it was Hines or Nunzio or anybody else, it seemed to Norah that Gilda would have done anything in the world to keep her husband from finding out.

On to the next step: Suppose Valente had found out that Gilda was unfaithful. Would he have used Nunzio as the instrument of his revenge while he sat snowbound in his country retreat? Could it have been Nunzio who committed the murder at his order?

Would Valente give the secretary that kind of power over him?

Never.

Could Nunzio have betrayed his boss and done it on the order of a rival gang? That could not be ruled out. In the intimate inner circle around Valente there was nobody else. Except:

Armanda Sequi.

The old lady had been with her friend, Giustina di Lucca, in the Bronx from 6:00 P.M. to just before midnight. The whole di Lucca family supported her, indignant that Mrs. Sequi should come under suspicion. The investigating officer, Nicolo Tedesco, had been obliged to hear the story of how Armanda Sequi had taken the young, orphaned Gilda into her home and raised her as her own all over again. He had to listen to how Armanda Sequi loved Gilda, idolized her, had built her entire life around her.

What about the life Gilda had led away from her husband and his aunt? What about the young people she had supported, who depended on her for their livelihood and future? One was left:

Mary Ruth Rae.

She had no alibi for the pertinent times—not for the night of Gilda Valente's drowning, nor for the time her ex-roommate went out the window, nor for when Peter Hines was beaten and smothered. One could posit that both Davies and Hines were killed in order to silence them, but why should Mary Ruth kill Gilda? Gilda was making it possible for the country and gospel singer to realize a dream. She had been supporting her in a style to which Mary Ruth had never even aspired.

There was no one else. For all her committees and parties, for all her lavish spending, Gilda and Dario Valente had few friends. Norah's pencil hovered. Who else? Could it be as the *capo* had suggested at the very beginning—that his wife was killed on the order of a rival gang? That meant an uncounted number of anonymous suspects. A dismaying prospect. Intimidating. But she had to deal with it. Up to now, Dario Valente had shown himself invulnerable to his enemies, so maybe they had tried to reach him through his wife. He loved Gilda; he had been inordinately proud of her—of her beauty, of her acceptance by society. By hurting her, his enemies could wound him deeply, but not destroy him.

It was a dark morning and growing darker. A yellow haze presaging another storm smothered the city. The lights in the squad room were turned on, but Norah didn't move to turn her own on. The shadows were heavy around her, but she was unaware of them. Wyler came to her door and thought she wasn't in. He asked Art Potts. Potts knew she was there, but advised against disturbing her.

The heaviness of the atmosphere intensified the depression Norah felt. She recognized Valente's emotional dependence on his young wife. His enemies, outside the law and within it too, couldn't destroy him by killing her, but if somehow they could have undermined his faith . . . if the hint that she had betrayed him could be passed on . . . Valente would not have been easy to convince, Norah thought. It would have taken more than a whisper meant to be overheard, a handkerchief carelessly given. Valente would recognize an Iago. He would not easily be duped. To be believed, to force him to act, the accusation would have had to come from someone close, someone he trusted completely.

Imogene Davies had known Gilda's secret and she was dead.

So was Peter Hines.

And Mary Ruth Rae? Certainly she was a part of Gilda's other life and she had run away. And Norah had let her go.

At last, Norah became aware of the darkness around her. The first few flakes of the next storm were floating lazily past her window. She shivered. The boiler must have broken down again, she thought; it always happened in the worst weather . . . Then she sat bolt upright. Phil Worgan had just reminded her how cold it had been in Peter Hines's apartment though apparently there had been steam in the building. She'd thought at the time that being a singer, Hines had turned off the steam to protect his throat from the dryness. She still thought so, but . . . it was there—amorphous—a sense of the truth.

She reached for the telephone.

Randall Tye was going over the lineup for the next show when his phone rang. He ignored it. He didn't take calls when he was working. They knew it at the switchboard. Somebody would pull the plug. But the phone went on ringing. In exasperation, he picked it up. "What?"

"Randall? It's Norah."

"Norah! What a nice surprise. I was going to call you, but I decided I should give you a little more time to . . . uh, miss me."

In spite of herself, Norah laughed. "I do miss you, Randall, more than I thought I would. But that's not why I called. I need a favor."

"Ah . . ." the newsman sighed. "This is against your code, isn't it? I thought you didn't believe in combining our two spheres."

"I was wrong."

"Okay. Tell me what you want." Randall Tye lit a cigarette, pushed his chair back from the typewriter, and listened to what Norah had to say.

When she was through, he took a couple more long, slow drags. "You really haven't told me a damn thing."

"I've told you as much as I can. I promise that when it's over I'll tell you the rest."

"You'll give me an exclusive?"

"I can't do that. You know I can't."

"You're asking me to book an unknown singer. Suppose she bombs?"

"She won't bomb. She has a reputation as a country singer." That was stretching it and she was sure that Randall knew it. "She's appeared in concert. She's auditioned for the Met."

"The concerts were paid for and the house papered. And the Met didn't hire her."

She hadn't expected him to be that well informed. "There are plenty of fine singers who aren't on the Met roster."

"You're asking me to take the whole thing on trust."

"That's right, I am."

"Okay, okay. So when do you want her up here?"

"Right away."

"Naturally. I'll squeeze her in on next Saturday."

"Make it this Saturday." She'd need some time to set it all up, Norah thought, but too long might allow the other participants second thoughts.

"You don't want much, do you?" Randall complained. "All right, all right, you've got it."

"Thanks, Randall. I knew I could count on you."

"Not so fast, Lieutenant. What are you going to do for me?"

Norah paused. "What do you want?"

Randall Tye laughed in the hollow manner of the old-fashioned movie villains as they twirled their mustaches at the cowering heroine. "However, I do have a second choice: dinner. If Mary Ruth is a disaster, dinner at your place."

"And if she's a hit?"

"Dinner. At your place."

"That's not fair."

"That's the deal. Take it or leave it."

"I'll take it."

Manny Jacoby shook his head.

"I can't buy it." He sighed. "Do you know how long we've been after this man? Organized Crime has been trying to link him to drugs and bribery and police corruption since way back before the Knapp Commission. They can't get him on prostitution or gambling. The IRS put its best examiners on him: nothing. Nothing sticks to him. Why? Because he's always had somebody else do the dirty work."

"Not this time," Norah replied. "This was one job Dario Valente could not afford to delegate."

"I don't see that. So his wife cheated on him. So she was carrying another man's child. He found out. Sure, it was a blow to his pride—to his honor—particularly after he'd taken the trouble to have the girl raised expressly to be his pure and unspoiled bride. No matter how much he loved her, he really had no choice but to have her killed. But no need to get blood on his own hands."

"Right. So that wasn't the reason he killed her. There had to be something more. Something worse. Something so shaming he couldn't risk turning the job over to anybody else for fear the secret might come out."

"I'd like to believe that," Jacoby said.

"It explains the other murders," Norah went on. "Both Imogene Davies and Peter Hines knew and had to be silenced."

"Just exactly what are we talking about here?"

"Lesbianism," Norah said.

Jacoby sighed heavily. "How are you going to get around the alibi?" he wanted to know. "Valente was out there in Bucks County under God knows how many feet of snow. People there, his neighbors, they saw him trudging to the airport. The airport manager confirms the time he arrived, and the pilot who flew him to New York supports the story. It checks out with personnel at the Pan Am heliport where they landed. The doctor who treated him says he was suffering from exposure and hypothermia. For God's sake, you saw him yourself."

"I know. Dario Valente based his alibi on the weather forecast."

Manny Jacoby folded his hands over his paunch, leaned back expectantly.

"Dario Valente could have called on any number of people to provide an alibi for him," Norah pointed out. "There are men and women who would be only too eager to do such a favor, but he didn't want that. He didn't want to be beholden, not for this. So he had to set up an alibi that would stand without anybody's help, that would not rest on anybody's word. He used the weather.

"A major snowstorm was predicted," she went on. "There were dire warnings at least thirty-six hours in advance. All Valente had to do was make it appear his wife was killed at a time when he was known to be in his country place—snowbound. The moment I walked out on that penthouse terrace and saw the body of Gilda Valente floating facedown in the pool, I thought what an odd way to commit murder in the middle of Manhattan. I wondered why it had been done in that particular manner. I didn't connect it with the storm."

"Did anybody check the pool thermostat that morning?"

"Yes. It was back to normal."

"Then how the hell are you going to prove it? Forget it, you can't."

Norah almost smiled; it was always *you* when the obstacle seemed insurmountable. "We have to show—first, what Gilda Valente was up to; then that Valente knew; finally, how he found out."

"Obviously, somebody told him."

They looked at each other, sharing the grave suspicion. Jacoby was the one who had to bring it into the open. "One of us?"

"I thought about that." Norah was relieved to be able to discuss it. "I thought maybe, after all these years of trying to nail Valente and failing, somebody, one of us, had finally found the chink in his armor, the one vulnerable spot—his love for his wife. When they got something on her, they leaked the information to him and sat back and waited for him to take action."

"Then why didn't they move right in on him? They could have caught him in the act."

"Because Dario Valente would not believe a rumor or even a direct accusation made by a cop or a Fed. Not from another Mafioso, either. Not that kind of an accusation."

Captain Jacoby was as eager as every man and woman in the department to nail Dario Valente and break his organization. There were times, he thought, when risks had to be taken. He could feel the hard knot forming in his stomach. "What do you have in mind?"

He listened, but it wasn't easy to suppress his natural skepticism.

"Will this Mary Ruth go along?"

"I'd like to fly down to Jacksonville myself to make sure."

Such a flight meant expense—a big bite out of the budget—and involved a lot of red tape. If they pulled it off, naturally nobody was going to criticize. But if they failed . . .

"Do what you have to do."

CHAPTER TWENTY

Norah returned from Jacksonville on Wednesday just before noon. She'd expected to be in much earlier, but weather had delayed the flight. She called Dario Valente from the airport, but he was not able to see her till evening. She decided it was probably as well. There were things to do and a couple of hours' sleep wouldn't hurt.

As soon as she entered the penthouse that night, Norah sensed a difference in the atmosphere. To start with, she was admitted by a maid, a plain, middle-aged woman in uniform, not by Salvatore Nunzio. There was no sign of Armanda Sequi. The maid escorted her to the living room and left her there. Spacious as it was, Norah felt confined. She decided it was because the drapes were drawn over the glass wall that overlooked the pool terrace. That shimmering blue water had been the focal point as well as an extension. Before Norah could go over and look out, Valente joined her.

"Well, Lieutenant, what can I do for you this time?"

"I have news for you, sir. I believe we are close to solving the crime. I know how your wife was killed."

"You say how; we all know she was drowned. I want to know—who?"

"I would like to conduct a final interrogation here, at the scene. With your permission, of course."

Valente's nobly hewn face was graven with a new network of lines already deeply set. "I'd given up hope," he told Norah. "And having given up, I find my desire for revenge has abated. Gilda is dead and nothing can change that. I would like to put my wife to rest and to rest myself. I want her body released for burial, Lieutenant, and then I want to forget."

"That, of course, is your privilege, Mr. Valente. You can request the body and I'm sure it will be released to you. I see no obstacle. And perhaps you can forget, but the police can't. I can't. As long as there's a possibility of finding the killer, we will pursue it. I would like your permission to bring the suspects here."

"You have more than one?"

"Yes. I want to conduct a reenactment here where the crime took place."

"I didn't think that was done anymore," Valente observed with a disparaging smile. "You really expect it to work?" He didn't wait for an answer. "Unfortunately, the pool is no longer in use. I intend to have it covered and turn the area into a greenhouse or a gym or . . . I don't know. Probably I'll end up selling the place."

"But you haven't done it yet?"

"The pool is covered, temporarily."

"May I see?"

At the touch of a button, the drapes parted. At another touch, a set of harsh working lights came on, revealing a desolate scene. The pool itself was covered by wooden slats. The brightly colored pillows were gone from the chairs and lounges. The shrubs were already wilted in their terra-cotta tubs. Tracks of the men who had laid the planking dirtied the terrazzo floor.

"Too many memories," the *capo* sighed.

"Could the cover be taken up and the pool filled for one night, Mr. Valente?" Norah asked. "You wouldn't have to be here yourself, if it would be too painful."

He considered. "You intend to trick the killer?"

"Entrapment is illegal, Mr. Valente, as you surely

know. It would get the case thrown out and defeat the purpose."

"No bugs," he warned. "No hidden cameras or anything like that. I won't have it. My people will make sure no electronic devices are planted anywhere for whatever purposes. Is that understood?"

"You have my word. Also, I'd like Mr. Nunzio and Mrs. Sequi to be present."

"All right. I'll be here too."

"As you wish." Norah nodded.

With that, Valente reached for the switch and flicked off the lights. Beyond the Plexiglas dome the stars gleamed bright in the winter sky. He looked up.

"My poor Gilda. She was a simple country girl. The pace of this city was too fast for her. There was too much pressure. I expected too much of her." He sighed again. "Too much."

It was set for that Friday at 10:00 P.M., the estimated time of Gilda Valente's death. Mary Ruth Rae, having eagerly accepted the invitation to appear on the Randall Tye show, would arrive at Kennedy at eight-thirty. Sergeant Arenas and Detective Tedesco would meet her at the airport and escort her directly to the penthouse. It was cutting it close, but Norah wanted to reduce the risk to the singer as much as possible.

One week before Christmas and the city glittered. It was cold, but the shoppers were flushed with the excitement of last-minute buying. The final round of parties was in full swing before the holiday assumed its family aspect and something of its religious significance. Before leaving her office, Norah Mulcahaney checked the airline: Flight 104A was on time.

There was no tree in the twenty-first-floor penthouse, no seasonal decorations, but the glamorous lure of the pool terrace had been restored. The planking had been taken up and the pool filled. The water sparkled with reflections of the artful lighting. Everything was clean, the plantings revived, the cushions back in place. Norah could almost see the slender yet voluptuous figure of Gilda Valente floating facedown in the center.

Norah made a slow tour of the area. "Does it seem the same?" she asked Valente. "What do you think?"

"I wasn't here," he reminded her. "It looks as usual."

"I want it the way it was that night. Could we have Mrs. Sequi and Mr. Nunzio in now? I'd like them to verify that everything is in place."

Valente picked up the nearest house phone and gave the order. "I hope all of this won't have been for nothing," he said to Norah.

"So do I. Has the manner of your wife's death troubled you, Mr. Valente? It has me."

"How do you mean?"

"Drowning somebody on the top of a roof in New York City isn't your usual MO. At the least, it suggests the killer was familiar with your home and with the layout."

"Obviously."

"What's not so obvious is why he chose drowning. Wouldn't knifing or shooting or even strangling have been easier? For one thing, to drown her he first had to get her into the water and then get in himself. I mean, it would have been difficult for the perpetrator to kneel at the edge and do it. She could just swim away, couldn't she?"

"Lieutenant, this is very painful for me."

"I'm sorry. Please bear with me a while longer."

"I'm running out of patience."

Norah didn't try to soothe him anymore. "Another problem for me was that the alibis don't mean much in this case."

Valente frowned. "Why do you say that?"

"Because of the weather, of course. Everyone was affected by it. By ten P.M., the time fixed for your wife's death, the city had come to a standstill. Theater performances, sports events, schools, meetings—all had been canceled. There was no surface transport. Even underground, the subways were without power from nine-thirty to just after eleven-thirty. In order to commit the crime, the killer had to be, if not actually in the building, then close by.

Very close. Afterward, his getaway would have been that much more difficult."

She paused, but Valente made no comment.

"However, if your wife died earlier, say between five and six, the whole situation changes. It had been snowing a couple of hours by then, but lightly, in flurries, and in the city there was as yet little accumulation. Movement was still normal. At that time, nobody in the case has an alibi. Your secretary, Salvatore Nunzio, was actually still here, in the study, working, at five-thirty. Mrs. Sequi had not yet left to visit her friend in the Bronx."

"You consider them suspects?" Valente was openly derisive.

"Both live in the building, and both have full access to this apartment; they can come and go at will. They were automatically suspects. Their alibis were strengthened by the weather conditions. But if the murder had been committed earlier, then they couldn't be eliminated. Nobody could. Not even you, Mr. Valente."

The *capo*'s face darkened. From beneath his hooded eyes he fixed Norah with a brief look of terrifying malevolence.

"You are wasting time in futile speculation, Lieutenant. Your medical examiner's report . . ."

He was interrupted by a light knock at the door, then Salvatore Nunzio and Armanda Sequi appeared together on the threshold. At a nod from Valente they entered.

"Lieutenant Mulcahaney wants to know if everything is as usual here," he told them, indicating the general area, then turned away as though the matter were of no interest to him.

"Specifically, I want to know if everything is as you remember it when you left on the night Mrs. Valente died," Norah corrected.

Nunzio answered first. "I couldn't say, Lieutenant. I wasn't in here that day or that evening. In fact, I seldom came in here at all. It was considered a part of Mr. and Mrs. Valente's private quarters. I've already made a statement to that effect," he reminded Norah in a manner that was easy and relaxed.

"Of course." Norah addressed Mrs. Sequi. "You supervised the restoring of this area and getting it ready for tonight?"

Vainly, the woman tried to catch Valente's eye for guidance, but he avoided her. "It seems as usual."

"Is it the way it was the morning you came up and discovered Mrs. Valente's body?" Norah asked. "Please look around once more, carefully. Take your time."

Valente remained as he was, back to them, staring up at the dome and the sky beyond.

"It's very difficult to remember," Armanda Sequi explained. "When I saw Gilda . . . when I realized . . . nothing else mattered. I didn't look around. I didn't see anything but . . . Gilda."

"Perhaps these pictures will refresh your memory. They were taken by the police photographer that morning. Please look through them." Norah waited while Mrs. Sequi shuffled them. "Do you see anything in those that is different, or perhaps is missing here tonight?"

"Ah, well, there's a bath towel on the chaise in these pictures." Armanda Sequi shrugged. "I didn't think to put one out."

"Would you do so now, please?"

Without attempting to consult Valente this time, Armanda Sequi went directly to a wall locker, opened it, and took out one of a stack of thick, blue-and-green-striped beach towels and placed it on the foot of the chaise nearest the edge of the pool.

"It's not like that in the photograph," Norah said.

The woman picked up the towel, unfolded it, and draped it across the chaise so that it was partially on the floor.

"Yes," Norah nodded. "But as I remember, the towel was damp. It must have been used, don't you think?"

Dario Valente spun around. "What in God's name has a damp towel got to do with it? I don't appreciate games,

Lieutenant. I've had enough. Say what you have to say and let's get it over."

"I'd like to do that, Mr. Valente. I'd like to reconstruct for you exactly what happened here on the night of the thirtieth, but you wouldn't accept it. That's why I've arranged for you to hear it directly from the person who was here that night with your wife."

"Her killer?"

"Her lover."

Norah was looking directly at Nunzio and, following her look, Valente laughed.

"Don't be ridiculous, Lieutenant. Salvatore knew what would happen if he so much as looked at Gilda once—the wrong way. As for Gilda, she had too much taste to look at him. Salvatore is my right hand. Smart, capable, reliable, but to my wife, he was a servant. You are totally on the wrong track, Lieutenant. You've wasted your time and mine." A firm knock at the door was further irritation. "Now what? Who've you got next, Lieutenant? All right, play out the scenario. Let's get it over with once and for all."

Challenge glittered in Valente's dark eyes but also curiosity. Then he smiled, and Norah knew that he believed he could meet and overcome whatever she had in store. She was counting on his arrogance. She opened the door.

Mary Ruth Rae stood proud in a black coachman's coat, her hair a flaming halo.

Valente stared. The blood drained out of his face. His eyes narrowed. "Who is this woman?"

"This is Mary Ruth Rae, a friend of your wife's. A very special friend."

Valente's eyes shifted to Armanda Sequi, a look so swift it would have escaped Norah except that she was anticipating it. When he looked back at her, Valente's eyes were red as a viper's. "I will not tolerate your obscene implications, Lieutenant. Get out of my house and take that . . . woman . . ."

"I loved Gilda. I'm not ashamed of it," Mary Ruth spoke in a clear, calm voice.

Valente gasped.

"How did she feel about you?" Norah asked.

"Gilda was lonely. For all her money and all her social activities, she was unfulfilled."

"How dare you!"

"Because she couldn't conceive." Mary Ruth Rae flinched at the *capo*'s rage but continued. "She wanted a baby so desperately. She was ashamed she couldn't get pregnant. She felt inadequate. She also felt rejected."

"I gave her everything."

"You bought her everything. She needed consolation, reassurance, affection. I tried to fill the void. I loved her. I wanted her to love me."

"Be quiet. I don't want to hear any more." He turned to Norah. "This is disgusting."

Armanda Sequi made a small whimpering sound and reached out a hand toward Valente, but at his lowering look pulled it back.

"She didn't want my love," Mary Ruth went on. "She wouldn't accept it. She wouldn't go beyond friendship. I was forced to be satisfied."

"She set you up in a luxurious apartment. She bought you clothes, hired a vocal coach for you," Norah pointed out.

"She did the same for other artists."

"Artists! She kept you as her whore!" Valente's cry was anguished.

Mary Ruth Rae blanched; tears welled up in her soft eyes. At last she was able to look directly at Valente. "We never had sex. You can believe that or not."

Norah broke in. "Nevertheless, when Gilda Valente learned that she was finally pregnant, she told you she wouldn't be seeing you anymore, isn't that right? Innocent or not, she didn't want to continue the relationship."

Valente groaned and covered his face.

"She was certain that once her husband learned she was actually pregnant at last, all would be well between them. She intended to drop all other interests and devote herself entirely to him and the baby. There could and would be no place in her life for you. In other words, she was going to cut you off."

"No, that's not true. She promised she'd continue to support my studies and take an interest in my career."

"She had no more interest in either and you knew it," Norah insisted. "You called; she wouldn't speak to you. You wrote; she didn't answer. Finally, on the thirtieth you managed to reach her and you threatened to tell her husband the child she was carrying wasn't his unless she agreed to see you. She told you to come over at six and to use the back way. She would leave both doors open for you.

"When you arrived Gilda was in the pool, naked."

Norah paused and every eye was drawn to the shimmering water. Each person there—Armanda Sequi, Salvatore Nunzio, Mary Ruth Rae, the detectives, and, above all, Dario Valente—had his own vision of the beautiful and seductive woman.

"You wanted her then as you'd never wanted her before," Norah suggested softly. "You were overwhelmed by desire. You stripped and got into the water with her. You thought if you took her right there and then, everything would be changed between you. But she fought you off. There was a struggle. She got her hands around your neck. You were choking and you fought back by pushing her under. You held her under too long."

Armanda Sequi's sobs punctuated the silence.

"Take her away," Valente told Norah. "Take her away."

"You didn't mean to kill her, did you, Mary Ruth?" Norah asked.

"I didn't kill her," the singer cried. "I did come here that night, that's true, but I didn't take my clothes off and get into the pool with her. I didn't push her under."

The redhead caught her breath, tried to calm down.

"Earlier that day Gilda told me she intended to devote herself exclusively to raising a family and that under the circumstances our friendship was no longer suitable. She could not go on sponsoring me and was withdrawing all financial support. She gave me six months to make other arrangements. I came here to plead with her. And I did end up threatening her. I did threaten to tell her husband that the child she was so proud to be carrying wasn't his. And do you know what her answer was?"

Mary Ruth Rae waited and Valente at last could do no less than raise his head and look at her.

"Gilda told me to go ahead and tell you anything I wanted. She said you would never believe it. She said you knew that she was totally loyal. That she would rather die than dishonor you."

"O Dio! Dio mio!" Armanda Sequi sobbed brokenly. She approached Valente timidly, reaching out as before and still not daring to touch him. *"Perdonami."*

"Basta. Taci."

"Perdonami, ti prego . . ." she entreated but he kept his face turned away. The woman could only appeal to the others. "I saw Gilda go into that apartment—with my own eyes. Time after time I followed her there. I waited outside. Sometimes for an hour, sometimes for a whole afternoon, till she came out again. A few minutes later, ten or fifteen usually, a man would come out after her, and sometimes a woman."

Armanda Sequi sighed heavily. "I didn't know what was going on. I could guess, but I had to be sure. There were only four apartments in the building—two art galleries, the office of an interior designer, and the other was that woman's," she said, pointing to Mary Ruth Rae. "But she was out most of the time when Gilda used the place." She sighed again. "So, I got hold of the cleaning woman and gave her money to let me take a look inside. Gilda's clothes were in the closet, her perfume on the dressing table, her underthings—that I had embroidered myself for her trousseau—were in the bureau drawers. It was a place of assignation."

She was breathing in short, shallow gasps, her right hand on her chest as though in pain. Norah made a move toward her, but was waved off.

"I was shocked, sickened. It was more than I could

bear. I confronted Gilda and I flung my accusations at her. She was gentle with me. She explained the apartment was for the use of the singers she was sponsoring and that she kept some of her things there as a convenience. I wouldn't listen. I preferred to believe the evil in my own mind."

"*Basta,*" Valente groaned. "Enough."

"It's my fault. It's all my fault. I did it. I killed her." She paused. She waited. She looked to the *capo,* but this time Valente didn't speak.

"I killed her," Armanda Sequi repeated. "My beautiful, spirited girl. I believed she had debased and degraded herself and brought shame on us all. Dario had entrusted her to my care and I had failed. I had to tell him. I had no choice. I meant to do it that night when he got back from the country. When I found out he wasn't coming back till the next day, I decided to make one last try to reason with Gilda. If she would give up the pretense of being a patron of the arts and close down that apartment, I would remain silent. I waited till I was sure the servants were gone and Salvatore too, then I came back upstairs and let myself in through the back.

"I was surprised to hear voices out here. The curtains were drawn, but I recognized Gilda's voice, of course, and the other voice was also a woman's. They were quarreling. Shouting. I couldn't understand much until the woman said to Gilda: 'I love you.' My head reeled. I think I lost consciousness. I'm not sure for how long. All I know is that when I recovered, everything was quiet.

"I peered through the curtains. Gilda was still in the pool, swimming lazily. She was alone. I came in. I had brought her up, nurtured her, loved her, but at that moment she was a stranger to me. I picked up the bath towel and called to her to come out."

The woman in the dowdy black dress and sensible shoes walked stiffly to the pool ladder. "I held the towel for her." She spread out her arms. "How many times had I wrapped my Gilda in a fresh, warm towel after her swim? How many times had I bathed her and held her in my arms as I patted her dry? She came to me as she always had, ex-

pecting warmth and love. As she came up the ladder out
of the water, I threw the towel over her head and pushed
her back. I kept the towel over her face so I wouldn't have
to look at her and so that her cries were muffled. I leaned
over and used all my weight to push her under and hold
her there. After a while, she stopped struggling." Armanda Sequi sighed deeply and was silent.

Valente went over to her, put his arm around her shoulders, and held her close. After a few moments, he leaned
over and kissed her gray head.

That's it? Norah thought. *He's going to let her take the
rap? Forget it, Mr. Valente.* What little sympathy she'd felt
for the man was washed away.

"How about the thermostat, Mrs. Sequi? The pool thermostat? When did you change the setting—before or
after?" she asked.

The woman looked up, bewildered.

Norah spoke to the *capo.* "I suggest, Mr. Valente, that
you already knew about your wife's transgressions long
before you went to your country house. I suggest that, in
fact, you went there to think over what you should do,
to render a verdict, and the verdict was—she had to die.

"When you first set eyes on Gilda, she was a beautiful
child on the verge of womanhood. The combination of her
beauty and innocence attracted you. You turned her over
to Mrs. Sequi to raise with the express purpose of keeping
her pure in body and mind till she was old enough to
marry. But she was already flawed. Her social activities
and her role as a sponsor of young artists were a means
of camouflaging her sexual escapades. Of course, you became suspicious. How could you help it with the money
that was pouring out? But you didn't want to believe what
your checkbook was telling you. And yet you couldn't ignore it. Hiring a detective was out of the question. You
couldn't put one of your own people on her; there was nobody you could trust to keep the secret. Besides, you were
too ashamed. But there was your aunt. She could watch
Gilda without arousing suspicion. She could listen to her

telephone conversations, intercept her mail. Follow her. She would tell you the truth and keep quiet about it."

Valente remained impassive. He neither protested nor commented. Only waited. So did they all, those present within the pool enclosure and those outside it—the *capo's* people and the police.

"Everything your aunt did was on your orders," Norah continued. "And what she found out was much worse than you had feared. Worse than a casual affair. It was devastating. But you believed what she told you."

Valente neither protested nor even flinched. He was proud, Norah thought. Could it be that his wife's homosexuality absolved him from responsibility in the failure of their marriage?

"So, Gilda had to be punished, and you had to do it yourself. You couldn't allow anyone else to touch her, or to know why she had been sentenced.

"You were due back here on Monday, but you called your wife early in the afternoon to tell her you wouldn't be home for dinner after all, but to expect you later on that night. You said you'd call her when you were leaving; that was to make sure she'd be here." And that, Norah thought, was the reason Gilda had allowed Mary Ruth to come over. "Naturally, you weren't at the house when you called. You were here, in the city, nearby. You waited till you were sure everybody had left for the night— servants, Nunzio, Mrs. Sequi, then you came in by the back too. It was probably close to six-thirty.

"Your wife was in the pool, naked. You confronted her. You demanded her lover's name. She denied everything." Norah paused. At this point she was recreating partly out of fact and partly instinct. She wondered how much farther she'd have to go.

"It was then she told you she was pregnant. You didn't believe it. You thought it was a last desperate attempt to distract you from your purpose. When she realized it wouldn't work, she got out of the pool and tried to run for it, but she couldn't get past you. You grabbed her. The two of you struggled and went down to the floor. She was biting, kicking, scratching. You, of course, had to be careful not to mark her, so you couldn't get free. The two of you fell into the pool together."

Dario Valente didn't move; nevertheless, Norah sensed an inner, increased alertness.

"You were determined to destroy the woman you had once loved and you were oblivious to her entreaties," she went on. "You paid no attention to what she tried to tell you. You had no pity for her pleading, her sputtering as she swallowed water, her desperate flailing to stay afloat. After a while, her resistance weakened and with the last gurgle of water and air in her throat, she died."

At last, Valente sighed, but he didn't challenge any of it.

"When you planned the murder, you didn't expect that your wife would already be in the pool. You thought it would be easy to overcome her and put her in the water and hold her under. After that, all you would have had to do was lower the pool thermostat and program it to return to its normal setting in the morning. That way the rate of decomposition of the body would be slowed, making it appear the time of death was much later. You would be able to drive back to your house before the roads became impassable. You would have an unassailable alibi.

"Finding Gilda already in the pool seemed a stroke of luck, even a sign that what you intended was an act of justice. But you hadn't expected her to offer so much resistance. She fought for her life. She pummeled and scratched and gouged. The cuts and bruises on your face that we all thought were sustained during your ordeal in the snow were in fact inflicted right here. Your wife dragged you, fully clothed, into the water with her. The struggle continued, and when it was over and you had prevailed, you came out in your soaking clothes, took them off, and wrapped yourself in the towel Gilda had placed on the chaise for her own use."

Norah indicated the towel she'd had Mrs. Sequi arrange there so carefully.

"Wrapped in the towel you carried your wet clothes

into your bedroom where you changed. The wet things you placed in a plastic bag to take with you. The towel, with which you had wiped yourself, you put back where you'd found it."

"Ah . . ." It was a long, low moan.

"Unfortunately, as it lay partially on the floor it sopped up additional water which had been splashed in the struggle. The lowered temperature of the water in the pool also brought down the air temperature, so the towel was still damp the next morning when your wife's body was discovered. The towel was analyzed routinely. In addition to the chlorinated water, there were also traces of blood—much diluted, but by present forensic methods more than enough to be analyzed."

He bowed his head.

"There's always something, Mr. Valente," Norah told him. "Always."

Still without replying, Dario Valente walked slowly toward a door on the far side of the wall, a door that gave access to the roof outside. Both Arenas and Tedesco cast a warning look at Norah.

"Mr. Valente," she called in a low but urgent tone.

He didn't look back, but at least he stopped where he was.

Norah took a tentative step toward him. "Mr. Valente . . ."

"Have no fear, Lieutenant." The *capo*'s heavy, handsome face was strained. "Jumping would be much too easy. I owe Gilda more than that."

CHAPTER
TWENTY-ONE

Dario Valente's expensive lawyers pleaded with him but couldn't make him hold his tongue. He spilled it all out. Catharsis. His guilt and remorse overwhelmed him. He was booked, arraigned, and denied bail principally because it was feared that left alone he might take his own life. On Rikers Island, he was placed under suicide watch. That was not what Norah feared. On the night of the arrest, he had been a few feet from the roof's edge and could have stepped out into emptiness. He could have ended it all right then. He hadn't, and for the reason he'd stated—that he had killed the only person in his life he'd ever loved and, as he believed, had killed her unjustly. He wanted to be punished. He welcomed every bit of the disgrace and humiliation.

Nevertheless, while Dario Valente willingly recounted the details of his wife's murder, confessed to pushing Imogene Davies out the window and ordering the death of Peter Hines, he would not speak regarding his other crimes or anything pertaining to the organization. Not one word. Not even an acknowledgment that there was an organization, much less his position in it. The district attorney of Manhattan and the U.S. attorney, Southern District, personally spent hours with the *capo*. FBI and NYPD interrogation teams worked in shifts. They sweated with exhaustion. They offered deals. They got nothing. And never would, Norah thought.

On the morning of Monday, December twenty-first, three weeks exactly after he drowned his beautiful young wife in the pool of their luxurious penthouse, Dario Valente, the youngest and most powerful of the crime bosses in the Northeast, was found hanging in his cell.

"So the mob finally got to him," Manny Jacoby remarked, the latest editions on the desk in front of him.

"I'd say so," Norah agreed. "And I'd say he was pretty much expecting it."

Jacoby propped his feet on a small stool he kept for the purpose. "There's going to be plenty of acrimony over how they did it." A slow smile tilted the corners of his pudgy mouth and his small eyes gleamed at the thought of the accusations that would be flying back and forth between the various services and the prison authorities. "At least we're out of it," he said smugly. "We did our job. We delivered. As far as we're concerned, the case is closed."

Norah licked her lips.

"Right, Lieutenant?"

"As a matter of fact, Captain . . ."

"No. Forget it. Whatever it is—and I'm not even going to ask—forget it. Let the FBI, Organized Crime, the DA, and the rest of them worry about it. Valente's death puts a big hole in his organization. We can take credit for that: the squad, the precinct, everybody. Everybody performed."

It wasn't often Manny Jacoby handed out praise. Norah recognized that was what it was.

"Thank you, Captain."

"The case is closed," he repeated.

"Yes, sir." She got up and went back to her office.

That Monday night, Armanda Sequi took a larger than usual dose of sleeping pills.

The next morning, when she didn't appear upstairs in

the penthouse, the daily maid knocked at her door. Getting no answer, she sought out Salvatore Nunzio. He got his spare set of keys and went in. First he notified 911, then he called Norah Mulcahaney directly.

Ordinarily, she would not turn out for an obvious suicide, but this was not an ordinary situation. Standing at the bedside of the elderly woman, looking down at the tranquil face that had been so tortured, Norah felt release of her own inner strain.

Yes, the case was closed—at last.

She prepared for the dinner with Randall Tye with great care. The menu particularly concerned Norah. Randall was accustomed to the very best gourmet food in expensive restaurants. No use trying to compete. She should fix something plain yet special. Irish stew, the way her father used to make it! Patrick Mulcahaney had taught Norah certain touches that Joe always said made the version memorable. It would be the perfect dish, she decided. Norah marketed, assembled, and cooked. While the stew simmered, she set the table, and then dressed. What to wear caused her almost as much deliberation. She settled for a mauve silk jumpsuit and with it she wore the aquamarine earrings that had been Joe's gift for their first anniversary.

The evening started well enough. Randall arrived punctually with flowers and wine. The flurry of dividing the massive bouquet between three vases and serving the drinks carried them past an initial awkwardness. By the time they reached the dinner table, Norah was forced to acknowledge it wasn't going well. Randall was subdued, thoughtful. Very little of his natural ebullience was in evidence. As dinner progressed, it was Norah who bore the burden of making conversation. Dessert finished, dishes cleared, they moved back to the living room for the coffee and liqueur.

"I warned you I wasn't much of a cook."

"You're an excellent cook. Everything was delicious."

Tye raised the liqueur glass with its golden liquid. "To Mary Ruth Rae, who made this possible."

Norah smiled. This, at least, was a safe topic. "She was a big hit, wasn't she?"

"Absolutely. We'll have her back. And she'll get other offers, plenty of them." He didn't smile.

"All right, Randall, what's the matter?" Norah asked. "You've been glum all evening. Something bothering you?"

"As a matter of fact, yes. I have a question."

"Ask."

"You told me you needed to get Mary Ruth back to New York to testify. You said she would resist coming back, but that the offer of a guest appearance on the show would tempt her."

"That's right."

"But that wasn't the real reason you wanted her up here."

"It was, ultimately. Before that, I needed her help to break Valente."

"You used her."

"There wasn't any other way. She understood that. She agreed to do it."

"How much of the story she told Valente about the night of the murder was true?"

Norah hesitated. "Off the record?"

Randall scowled. "What choice do I have? Okay."

"Most of it was true. Mary Ruth did call Gilda and ask to see her and Gilda agreed. She dismissed the servants early and received Mary Ruth while in the pool—naked. Doesn't that suggest something?"

Tye's eyes widened. "That Gilda was the seductress?"

"Oh, I think so. She initiated the relationship with Imogene, then Peter Hines, and finally with Mary Ruth. But we had to make Dario Valente believe the exact opposite. We had to make him see Mary Ruth as the aggressor and Gilda as the innocent victim of her shameful desire. We had to convince him that he had made a terrible mistake. In the process we had to convince Armanda Sequi too.

It was possible only because they both loved her and in spite of everything wanted to believe in her innocence."

But Tye was not convinced. "You took a big chance. Suppose it hadn't worked? He could have ordered Mary Ruth killed like he did Davies and Hines."

"He wasn't responsible for their deaths."

"He admitted it."

"Why not? He had nothing more to lose."

Randall Tye frowned. "Then who? The old lady?" He was openly disparaging.

"Don't underestimate the old lady. Armanda Sequi was as strong and ruthless as Valente and when it came to Gilda, a lot more clear-sighted. She knew her young charge very well. The girl was already sexually mature when he put her in Sequi's charge, and it was all she could do to keep Gilda out of trouble. Naturally, she didn't tell Valente. He wouldn't have married Gilda and he would have withdrawn his financial support. It would have been the end of the small comforts that eased Armanda's poverty and the end of all the dreams of the luxury to come. Maybe she hoped that once married Gilda's needs would be fulfilled. It wasn't long before she realized it wasn't working out that way. Armanda Sequi had been keeping close watch on Gilda long before Valente summoned her. She knew about Davies and Hines, though probably she didn't fully understand the ambivalence of the relationships till later.

"With Gilda dead, she thought the secret was safe. Then the police investigation began. Every time I called at the penthouse Mrs. Sequi was there in the background—a shadow, but present. Watching. Listening. Having deceived Valente in the first place, she was now determined to protect his honor. To do that, all those who knew Gilda's secret had to be silenced. Davies was no trouble; Sequi was physically stronger. As for Hines, she heard Valente promise he would find Hines and turn him over to us. She knew Valente would have him worked over first. I don't know how she found out exactly when it happened, maybe Valente told her, but she went over there soon after. Hines was barely alive. It didn't take much strength to hold a pillow over his face till he stopped breathing."

Tye sighed.

"Mary Ruth got away in time, but the threat still hung over her and always would. The best way to protect her was to bring the relationship out into the open, but to have her pose as the instigator."

"So Sequi killed herself out of remorse."

Norah shook her head. "I doubt it. From her point of view, Davies and Hines deserved to die. No, I think it was the possibility of Gilda's innocence that gnawed at her. That the baby she carried might, after all, have been Dario's. That's what destroyed them both."

Randall Tye reached for Norah's hand and looked into her eyes. "I should have known better. I apologize."

"Accepted."

He raised her hand, turned it palm up, and kissed deep within its hollow.

"Now, about your cooking . . ."

The phone rang.

"Just in time." Norah jumped up, grinning. She was gone only a few minutes, but when she came back she wasn't smiling anymore.

"Something wrong?"

"That was John Douvas, the ADA in charge of the Altman case. They've decided to drop the murder charge."

"Well! That's good news, isn't it? That's what you wanted."

"Yes," Norah said, but the frown remained. "The charges for illegal possession and for reckless endangerment will stand."

"In other words, she'll be tried for shooting Pesrow in the leg and he'll go ahead with his case against you and the department."

"It was all so simple back when I joined the force," Norah told him. "The cop was supposed to protect the victim and apprehend the criminal. The court was supposed to mete out the punishment. Now it's all mixed up.

The criminal claims to be the victim and challenges the cop, who goes to trial to justify doing his job. The victim is left to fend for himself."

She pursed her lips and shook her head. "I never thought it would be like this."

"I never thought you'd give up," Tye chided.

Norah raised her head. Her blue eyes were steady and gleaming. She squared her chin. "Who said anything about giving up?"

About the Author

Lillian O'Donnell lives in New York City. She has been an actress and dancer and was the first woman stage manager in the New York theater.

Lillian O'Donnell

Absorbing mysteries from start to finish.

12